FOR THIS LIFE ONLY

Also by Stacey Kade

Novels for Young Adults
The Ghost and the Goth
Queen of the Dead
Body & Soul
Project Paper Doll: The Rules
Project Paper Doll: The Hunt
Project Paper Doll: The Trials

Novels for Adults
Bitter Pill
738 Days

FOR THIS LIFE ONLY

STACEY KADE

SIMON & SCHUSTER BFYR

NEW YORK LONDON TORONTO SYDNEY NEW DELHI

An imprint of Simon & Schuster Children's Publishing Division

1230 Avenue of the Americas, New York, New York 10020

SIMON & SCHUSTER BFYR is a trademark of Simon & Schuster, Inc.

For information about special discounts for bulk purchases, please contact Simon & Schuster Special Sales at 1-866-506-1949 or business@simonandschuster.com.

The Simon & Schuster Speakers Bureau can bring authors to your live event. For more information or to book an event, contact the Simon & Schuster Speakers Bureau at 1-866-248-3049 or visit our website at www.simonspeakers.com.

Jacket design by Krista Vossen

Interior design by Hilary Zarycky

The text for this book was set in New Baskerville.

Manufactured in the United States of America

First Edition

2 4 6 8 10 9 7 5 3 1

Library of Congress Cataloging-in-Publication Data

Names: Kade, Stacey.

Title: For this life only / Stacey Kade.

Description: New York : Simon & Schuster Books for Young Readers, 2016. | Summary: "A young man struggles to move forward after the death of his twin brother in this contemporary novel about loss, redemption, and love"— Provided by publisher.

Identifiers: LCCN 2015039687| ISBN 9781481432481 (hardback) | ISBN 9781481432504 (eBook)

Subjects: | CYAC: Death—Fiction. | Grief—Fiction. | Brothers—Fiction. | Twins—Fiction. | Love—Fiction. | BISAC: JUVENILE FICTION / Social Issues / Death & Dying. | JUVENILE FICTION / Social Issues / Dating & Sex. | JUVENILE FICTION / Social Issues / Values & Virtues. |

Classification: LCC PZ7.K116463 Fo 2016 | DDC [Fic]—dc23

LC record available at http://lccn.loc.gov/2015039687

To Becky, my oldest friend (in duration, not age).
My life literally would not be the same if I hadn't met you.
I have no idea what moved you to reach out to the quiet and
slightly strange girl on your freshman wing in Lankenau,
but this quiet and slightly strange girl thanks you.

FOR THIS LIFE ONLY

CHAPTER ONE

ACCORDING TO MY DAD, Christmastime is family time. But after eleven straight days at home, I can tell you, it starts to feel a little more like prison time. I love my family, but there's only so much togetherness any sane person can stand.

And now, postdinner on a Saturday night, staring down the barrel of day twelve, I was ready to crawl out of my skin to see someone I wasn't related to.

"You have to let me take the Jeep tonight," I said, pushing open Eli's door without bothering to knock.

"What?" Perched on the edge of the bed, Eli slammed his nightstand drawer shut, a fleeting look of guilt on his face. Our face, technically, since we were identical. Blond hair, blue eyes, and ears that stuck out a little too far—that was us.

"What are you doing?" I asked, frowning at him.

"Nothing." Eli stood and pushed past me, heading toward the bathroom. "And forget it. I have stuff to do tonight."

"Right." I snorted, following him. "Like Leah?"

He paused to look over his shoulder at me, his mouth a tight line.

"Oh, come on, I was kidding!" I protested.

Okay, so maybe antagonizing Eli about his perfectly perfect girlfriend wasn't the best way to go about getting a favor, tempting as it was. The two of them were made for each other: the pastor's good son and the church council president's daughter who wanted to be a missionary. But they were also both rule-followers to the extreme and annoyingly exacting on themselves and everyone else.

Hey, whatever worked for them. I wasn't the one not-sleeping with her.

"Why don't you—" Eli began, as he flipped on the bathroom light.

"I can't ask Zach. Everybody's already over there." I leaned in the doorway, while Eli rummaged in the medicine cabinet. "I can drop you off at Leah's on the way," I offered.

The dusty pine smell of the drying-out Christmas tree downstairs mixed with the cinnamon candles my mom insisted on burning for "holiday ambience" was starting to get to me. Made me feel like the walls were closing in. I needed to be somewhere where I could breathe and be myself, even if it was only for a few hours.

"I said no."

I raised my eyebrows. "Seriously?"

He pulled drawers open and slammed them shut, looking for something.

"Fine," I said. "Then ask Leah to come get you. She has a car, right?"

He shook his head. "It's not fair to ask her to do that—"

"At the last minute, I know. But it's also not fair that we have to share a car when she could be using hers to get you," I pressed. "Division of resources or whatever."

"Not everything is about you, Jace," Eli said. Then he scowled. "Sarah!" he bellowed. "You left the toothpaste cap off." He pulled the capless and nearly flat toothpaste tube from Sarah's drawer. "Again!"

I stared at him. "What's wrong with you?" This was not my normally-even-tempered-to-the-extreme brother.

"It makes a mess, and it's gross. I hate that," he muttered.

"Jesus says not to hate." Sarah arrived in the doorway in time to make the pronouncement in her best Sunday-school-student voice. Her reddish-blond hair was sticking up in all directions, with a Disney Princess hair-thingy clinging for dear life on the side. She'd probably been pretending to be a pony again, which usually involved placing a blanket over her head as a mane.

"Yeah, well, I'm pretty sure Jesus would have been a proponent of putting the cap back on." Eli loaded toothpaste on his brush with a grimace.

"Actually, I'm pretty sure clumpy toothpaste wouldn't have been an issue. Son of God, water into wine and all," I pointed out quickly, in the name of keeping the peace and getting back to the main point. Me, taking the Jeep.

"See?" Sarah stuck her tongue out at Eli, and he rolled his eyes at her.

"E, please," I said. "I'm begging you. Mom is talking about another round of family Scrabble, and Sarah cheats more than I do. I can't take it."

"I do not cheat!" Sarah folded her arms across her chest, her lower lip jutting out. "I'm six. I don't know as many words as you do."

"You know better than to spell 'cat' with a 'q,'" I said. She'd gotten away with it because my parents thought it was adorable.

She gave me a sly grin. "Maybe."

"See? Cheater." I ruffled her hair further, and she squealed in mock protest.

Eli paused in brushing his teeth. "Won't Kylie be there?" he asked me quietly, around a mouthful of foam.

In spite of myself, I stiffened. "Probably."

He spat in the sink and rinsed his brush. "If you just talked to her—"

I grabbed the hand towel off the ring on the wall and chucked it at the side of his head.

"You missed a spot," I said, gesturing to the glob of toothpaste at the corner of his mouth. He'd go out like that if I didn't stop him. And it was bad enough that he was wearing his church camp T-shirt out in public. I could see the big block letters of last year's theme and Bible verse on the back through his button-down.

SEE YOU ON THE OTHER SIDE
For God so loved the world, that he gave his only Son, that whoever believes in him should not perish but have eternal life.
John 3:16

"Kylie doesn't come over anymore," Sarah said. "Why not? I liked her."

"Aren't you supposed to be getting your pajamas on?" Eli asked Sarah as he wiped his mouth. He took his role as the oldest—three minutes ahead of me—a little too seriously sometimes. Though in this case, I appreciated the diversion.

"You're not Mom or Dad," Sarah said. "You can't tell me what to do." Then she turned her attention back to me. "Did Kylie die?" she asked with a curiosity that bordered on weird and/or inappropriate. "Did God kill her?"

I groaned. A couple of weeks ago, my mom had taken Sarah to the funeral and graveside service of a longtime church member, Mrs. Gallagher. Normally we didn't get dragged to funerals, even the ones my dad presided over, but because my mom had to be there and Eli and I were in school, Sarah had to go. It was her first one.

Apparently, my dad had used the standard language about God calling a church member home, and that somehow got twisted in Sarah's brain. Since then, she kept popping up with these really bizarre questions about death and dying.

"Sarah, death is nothing to fear," Eli said. "If you listen to the scriptures, you'll see that Jesus talks about going ahead of us—"

I made an impatient noise. "When you die, you go toward the bright light, and Jesus and the rest of us will be there, waiting for you. Then everyone is in heaven and it's all good. End of story."

Eli sighed. "That's not really doctrinally—"

I rolled my eyes. "Kylie is fine," I said to Sarah. "She decided she liked the guys better at St. Luke's is all."

Sarah frowned. "Why?"

"I don't know, Sares." And right now, I didn't care. At least, not as much. I'd rather take the risk of running into my ex-girlfriend at a party than stay in one more night.

"That's not nice," Sarah said after a moment of contemplation.

"Gotta agree with you there," I said, and she tackled my leg in a sideways hug.

With another heavy sigh, Eli regarded both of us, his expression relenting. "Okay," he said, hanging the hand towel in the ring on the wall.

I straightened up. "I can have the—"

"I'll drop you off," he said. "But you have to tell Mom and Dad and find your own way home."

"Got it, not a problem," I said, relieved. Though I might have been overestimating the ease with which I'd accomplish both of those things. But one obstacle at a time.

"Jace, you should stay home," Sarah whined, clinging to my leg. "It's Christmas."

"Nope," I said. "Not anymore." Thank God.

My parents had a ritual for the Saturday evenings that weren't filled with wedding receptions, fund-raiser potlucks, or emergency calls. One glass of wine apiece, a big bowl of popcorn to share, and an old movie that would end by ten so my dad could be up and at the church by six a.m.

"Everything's ready for tomorrow?" my dad asked from

the couch, lowering the remote to focus his attention on Eli as soon as we rounded the corner into the family room.

Technically, we were both working at the church as interns this year, but everyone knew Eli was more into it than I was. Scratch that; he was into it and I wanted out of it. He would be the one to join my dad at the church as soon as he was done with college and seminary. Good for him, not for me.

"Yes. Did a mic check and replaced the batteries in your pack. Delores said Carey Daniels called in sick for acolyting, so I called down the sub list until I got someone. And the staple cartridge was replaced this afternoon, so the bulletins for all three services are done."

Dad nodded. "Good."

"Jacob?" my mom asked from her corner of the couch, taking in my jacket with a frown.

"Eli's going to drop me off at Zach's," I said.

"I thought we were going to do a final round of Scrabble." She gestured to the game set up on the coffee table. "We've already got the first Indiana Jones queued up. Sarah will be in bed before the face-melting part." The last was said in a pseudo-whisper.

"I heard that," Sarah shouted from upstairs. "I want to see!" Yep, that was my sister.

"Maybe tomorrow after church?" I offered to my mom, resisting the urge to shift my weight from foot to foot.

My dad sighed and sat up, moving to the edge of the couch.

I braced myself for the coming lecture.

"Jacob, if you're going out, don't give me a reason to hear bad reports. No drinking, no carousing, no breaking town curfew. Appearances are important. Because no matter how well you think you know everyone there . . ."

"Someone is always watching," Eli and I recited obediently, though my teeth were clenched.

"Exactly. And we have an obligation to be good examples." Theoretically, my dad was speaking to both of us, but his gaze was focused on me.

Because I was the one trying to have a life outside the church, to be someone other than just the pastor's less-good son.

It was something outsiders never understood. We didn't get to be individuals. We were Pastor Micah's family, a portfolio of my dad's work, shining examples of his leadership, his discipline, his faith at work in his own home. Our successes were his. Our mistakes—from a wrinkled shirt to a failing grade—were potential watch signs of trouble within the ministry.

God, as my dad's vague omnipresent "boss," might be forgiving, but the members of Riverwoods Bible Church weren't always so open-minded.

I was the "troubled one," by virtue of breaking curfew

a few times, getting busted at *one* party my freshman year, achieving lower grades than my twin, and generally being less involved in Riverwoods than Eli. (If there was a Bible study, he was a part of it.)

In other words, normal crap, stuff that would probably earn a week or two of grounding or maybe only a raised eyebrow and a scolding in a regular family.

But we weren't regular, unfortunately.

For the grades, my parents got me a tutor, and for the lack of involvement, they stuck me in the joint internship with Eli. But for the curfew violations and the party, my dad had enlisted me in community service at the Riverwoods food pantry for months. Part of that whole "being a good example" thing. I'd just finished paying for my last infraction. And with baseball practice starting up again in a couple of months, I did not want another session.

In a year and a half, I'd be done, out of here. On a baseball scholarship, I hoped, to somewhere else, where I wouldn't have to worry about anybody but me.

"Jace will be fine," Eli said with a confident nod at my dad, and I felt a rush of gratitude toward my brother, for extending his good credit over me. Whatever had been bugging him earlier seemed to be gone now. "Don't worry."

As always, Eli's casual word was more convincing than

my most earnest promises. Not that I bothered to make them very often anymore.

"Home by ten thirty," my dad said, pointing the remote at me. "Not a second later. You need to be at early service at least fifteen minutes before the prelude."

"Of course," I said quickly. Although at that point, I would have agreed to anything to get out.

CHAPTER TWO

TWO HOURS LATER, THE front half of me was sweating by the bonfire, while my back half was freezing, the raggedy barn on Zach's family's back forty not doing nearly enough to block the wind. And my beer was mostly foam.

It was the most relaxed I'd felt in days.

I tipped my cup and poured the excess head to the dirt-packed ground before the fire.

"Too much for you, PK?" Caleb asked with a snort.

I flipped my middle finger at him, which never failed to elicit an "oooh" of pretend shock from our shortstop. He loved to make a big deal out of me being a "preacher's kid."

"So listen. I heard Randle is out," Derek said from his position on a log deemed too large for firewood. His girlfriend, Lacey, shivered next to him, despite the multiple blankets over her shoulders. It was warmer than it had been for days, right at freezing, but that wasn't saying much.

I stared at him. "Are you serious?"

"Yep, grades. He's failing calculus. My cousin goes to school with him."

"Parkland will never make it without him," Caleb said, a huge shit-eating grin spreading across his face. "State is ours."

"Maybe, maybe not," Derek said, but I could hear the carefully contained excitement in our captain's voice. "Depends on if we can keep it together this year." He narrowed his eyes at us.

A trip to state might mean more scouts, better scholarships. As a left-handed pitcher, I had some interest already, but last year had screwed us up. Two of our seniors had been benched for the final four games of the season, which killed our record.

"Man, that wasn't us." Matt, our first baseman, chucked his cup into the fire, where it immediately sent up spirals of black, toxic-smelling smoke.

"Doug and Aaron were just messing around. It's not our fault that Thera chick can't take a joke," Caleb insisted.

"She probably made it up for the attention," I said. "Or to be a pain in the ass." Thera Catoulus's mom was Psychic Mary, the one and only fortune-teller in town. They lived in one of those crappy little houses, with a neon hand in the window and walk-in pricing listed by the front door.

The house happened to be right across from River-woods' original church building, where we held traditional early morning services on Sunday and the smaller services during the year.

Overgrown lawn, shitty piles of old tires dumped by the porch, and that blinking neon sign in the window advertising "occult services"—all just fifty feet away from Riverwoods' pristine stone steps.

It drove my dad crazy, which meant we had to hear about it. All the time. Plus, there was a superconservative contingent within Riverwoods—some of them, like Leah's dad, were even on the council—and they kicked up a congregation-wide tantrum every once in a while about satanism and the devil literally being on our doorstep.

My dad had tried to buy Psychic Mary out when Riverwoods built the new building, the auditorium, but she had refused.

So the auditorium was actually a block and a half from the original sanctuary, which made parking a bitch. And every time a parishioner complained, my dad would come home in a superpissy mood. That was fun.

"I don't know," Lacey said quietly.

Everyone stared at her.

"You believe her?" Caleb asked with a sneer.

"No . . . I don't know," Lacey said, curling deeper into

her blankets. "I just don't think that your coach would have benched them for nothing. I mean—"

"It doesn't matter," Derek said. "We need to focus on this season. That means keeping our noses clean and staying away from trouble. Any kind of trouble." He tipped his cup in my direction.

"Yeah," I muttered. My dad's strictness and punishments were legendary. And he wouldn't care if I missed practices or if the team was hurt by my absence. That counted as "something you should have thought of before."

My dad didn't have time to go to most of my games. It wasn't only me, though. He missed Eli's debate team events too sometimes, and Sarah's piano recitals. The church always came first.

Whatever. It's not like it mattered. Okay, maybe a little. But only because maybe if he saw what it meant to me, if he saw that I *belonged* on the field, then maybe he wouldn't have been so quick to try to take it away.

When I was on the mound, I felt whole in a way I didn't in any other place. It was in the smell of the grass and the dirt, the warmth of the sun on my back in those late afternoon practices, how it felt when the ball left my hand just right and I could tell it was going straight to the catcher. Like there was a magnet between the ball and his mitt. Destiny.

My dad was proud of me, of all of us, but it was like in

this general, generic way. He didn't know my stats or that I struggled with my circle changeup and was contemplating switching to the Vulcan. With too many competing River-woods priorities, he didn't have space in his brain for that kind of information.

Movement on the other side of the fire caught my attention. Kylie approached the outer edge of the light, her puffy white coat bright in the surrounding dimness. Her dark hair was mostly stuffed under a blue-and-gray beanie, the one I'd given her for her birthday last year. We were friends first. Her brother, Scott, was our center fielder, so she'd been hanging around team events for years.

That only made it worse when she dumped my ass last month at a party after telling me "it's not working." But lately, for some reason, she kept wanting to talk to me, to explain. To try to make things better. How exactly was talking going to make it better? Especially when she was with that dude from St. Luke's? She'd brought him tonight. I could see him talking to Scott behind her.

No thanks.

Kylie gave a tentative wave in my direction, her red cup clutched in her other hand.

I turned away and took three big swallows to finish my beer. "I should probably be getting home," I said to Derek, chucking my cup into the fire.

"Pussy," Caleb coughed into his fist.

I ignored him. "Anyone seen Zach?"

Lacey pointed to a dim corner of the barn, where I could barely make out two figures, arguing quietly with wild hand gestures and wobbly balance. A glass bottle of some kind of liquor was on the ground nearby, the side of it flickering with the reflection of firelight. "Um, he and Audrey are . . ."

Damn it. My best friend was always DD because he didn't drink. Except when he and his on-again, off-again girlfriend were fighting.

"I can take you home," Kylie offered, her voice carrying a little too loud across the fire. "I haven't touched my beer yet, and Dylan has his car—"

"I've got it," I muttered. I'd get Zach's keys and borrow his car. I'd only had a couple, and not even full cups because Caleb didn't know how to fucking pour.

Turning on my heel, I moved away from the fire and headed into the barn.

"Zach," I shouted, giving plenty of advance warning in case there was some deeply personal shit going on. I'd been present for their fights before, and Audrey didn't filter much when she was pissed. I'd heard plenty about their sex life. And I didn't need to know that much about either one of them. "Keys, bro."

Audrey gave an exaggerated huff at the interruption.

"One sec," Zach said to her before turning to me, half stumbling with movement. "You've been drinking."

I rolled my eyes. "Less than you," I pointed out. "I'm fine."

He squinted at me blearily. "Are you sure? You could stay here. Everyone else is."

Everyone including Kylie and her boyfriend? Hell, no.

I didn't feel the same way about her anymore. It would be hard to after getting my heart stomped on with such force and precision, but that didn't mean I wanted to hang out with her or, worse yet, try to dodge her various "we need to talk" attempts through the whole night.

Why couldn't she do the normal thing and pretend we never knew each other?

"I have to get home. Now," I said to Zach. "Church tomorrow, remember?" It would be difficult enough to explain why I had Zach's car; I didn't want to be late too.

He nodded after a second, a delayed reaction, and then pulled his keys from his pocket and tossed them to me. "Your mouthwash is in the glove box from last time."

I caught his sloppy toss one-handed, snatching the keys out of the air and turning to . . .

. . . charge smack into Kylie, who'd evidently followed me.

On impact, her red plastic cup, caught between us, gave a loud crack and I felt the cold slop of liquid against my chest.

A quick look down revealed beer in a large, spreading

stain on my red T-shirt and sprayed across the left side of my coat.

"Oh, my God, Jace, I'm so sorry." She wiped her hand on her jacket and tried to reach for me.

I moved out of her reach, holding my dripping shirt away from me before trying to wring it out. Beer dribbled out from between my fingers and onto the ground, but not enough. I could feel it soaking the long-sleeved shirt I had underneath as well. Even if I took off my coat and managed to get dry, the smell would still be too strong.

A voice in the back of my head began to chant *shit, shit, shit* with an ever-increasing degree of panic.

"I wanted to make sure you—" Kylie began.

"It's fine," I said sharply. "I'm fine. Just stop."

Hurt flickered across her face before she turned and stalked away, but I ignored her in favor of bigger problems.

I was screwed.

It was risky enough to drive after a couple of beers when I was four years from legal, but getting behind the wheel smelling like the Wrigley bleachers after a particularly disheartening Cubs loss was a monumentally bad idea. And even if I made it home without getting pulled over, there was no way I was getting past my parents.

Not without help. That only left me with one option.

Fuck.

• • •

The rumble of the deteriorating muffler on our Jeep Cherokee was distinctive enough that I heard Eli coming a mile away and was reaching for the door handle before he came to a complete stop.

"What took you so long?" I asked, my teeth chattering. "Did Mom and Dad give you crap about coming to get me?" The outer shell of my coat was stiff in patches where the beer had soaked in and then frozen. I had no idea what temperature beer froze at, but away from the shelter of the barn and the bonfire, I'd found it.

"I think the standard response is actually 'thank you,'" Eli said.

I slid in and yanked the door shut after me, cutting off the distant sounds of the party behind me.

"Right. Sorry, thanks." Not bothering with my seat belt, I stripped out of my jacket, shivering despite the heat blasting out of the vents in the ancient Jeep.

Eli nodded, a tight movement that told me he was a little exasperated with me. It was exhausting being the good and responsible one all the time. Or so I assumed.

"Did you bring me a shirt?" I asked.

He pointed toward the backseat.

"Thanks." I twisted in my seat and grabbed for the neatly folded clothing. "Seriously?" I asked, holding up his debate team sweatshirt. BIG TALK, BIG WALK was emblazoned across the front in embarrassingly huge letters. It was almost as bad as his church camp T-shirt.

"It's all I had with me."

I pulled my beer-soaked shirts over my head and dropped them to the plastic floor mat next to my jacket. I'd have to find a way to slip them all into the laundry later. "Dude, my room is right—"

"I wasn't at home," he said.

That surprised me. I paused with his sweatshirt halfway over my head. I was usually the one cutting it close to curfew. Eli was always home in plenty of time. "Where were you?" No way he was still at Leah's this late. Her curfew was even earlier than ours.

He didn't answer right away, concentrating on the shiny black ribbon of road and driving exactly three miles an hour below the speed limit, and I finished pulling on the sweatshirt.

"How do you know the right thing to do?" he asked finally, his fingers fidgeting on the wheel. "When both options mean hurting people, I mean."

I stared at him. His shoulders were slumped forward, making him almost hunched over the wheel. "Are you cheating on Leah?" I asked.

"No! Just forget it." Eli accelerated slightly, as if by speeding he could leave the conversation behind.

I'd never seen him like this before. "No, no, wait." I

held up my hand. "What's going on? Is this what was bugging you earlier?"

Eli sighed. "Sorry. I can't . . ." He hesitated. "Do you think there's a difference between doing the right thing that definitely hurts one person and doing the right thing that might hurt a lot of people?"

I felt the first dart of worry. "Eli, what are you—"

"I mean, in theory," he added.

I groaned. "It's Saturday, Eli. Come on. Take a night off."

Eli and my dad loved going round and round on heavy philosophical or religious issues. What is reality? How do we know what's real? How you do you define the greater good? I found it all mind-numbingly boring. Things weren't that complicated. Try not to be a crappy person. Go to church. Use your talents instead of burying them or whatever. If you do a good enough job, when you die, you go to heaven.

"I know what day it is," Eli said sharply.

"All right, so sorry, Touchy," I said, holding my hands up in surrender, which was usually enough to trigger a grouchy mumble or a reluctant smile.

But he didn't say anything.

With an impatient sigh, I turned in my seat to face him. "Look, E, no matter what's rolling around in that giant brain of yours, you have to know that you're on the right side of things. You always are. You're the good one, remember?"

I tried not to sound bitter. I mean, that was the deal with being half of a whole. Most of the time, what you were was in comparison to someone else. If one of us was good, the other was bad, simply by being less good.

Add to that the lore surrounding the children of ministers—you were either an innocent, naive angel or you were hell spawn, sent to test your parents' patience and dedication—and our roles were pretty much set. And yeah, okay, I'd made it my mission to make sure that my reputation wasn't exactly unearned.

Eli made a frustrated noise and braked to slow down as we crossed the bridge over the creek that ran through Zach's parents' land. "But that's just it. I don't know if I am. Have you ever . . ." He shook his head. "I guess some-times I wonder if the—"

Before he could finish his thought, the car gave a weird but distinct shimmy that made my stomach sink. Having put the car in the ditch once last year, I recog-nized the sensation instantly: the wheels had lost contact with the road.

Panic rose over me in a cold rush.

The moment slowed down to a crawl as we started to slide sideways. The antilock brakes kicked in with a hor-rible grinding noise, and Eli struggled with the wheel.

"Wait," he said, panicked. "Wait!" I wasn't sure who he was talking to.

"Turn into it!" I reached, for him, for the wheel. Both, maybe.

But it was too late for either.

The back end of the car hit the guardrail with an enormously loud crash of metal on metal, and then the guardrail gave. I felt the lurch of regular gravity retracting, abandoning us to our fate.

The sound of my heartbeat filled my ears, muting the chattering of the radio and the shriek of tearing metal as the Jeep rolled, turning our world upside down.

A bright blue umbrella, neatly folded and in its carrying sleeve, flew up from the floor somewhere with a rain of dirt and old receipts. The smell of burning plastic and oil was chokingly thick.

My body lifted up and out of the seat, in that sickening defiance of physics that felt familiar from roller coasters, and then I was thrown forward and sideways, with no restraint.

When my elbow connected with the dashboard, I heard a distinct crack. *That's bad. That's bad!*

And then I caught one last glimpse of Eli, his eyes wide and his face—our face—pale in the dashboard lights, as he spun away from me.

CHAPTER THREE

THE BEEPING—DISTINCT, RHYTHMIC, AND from some-where on my left—came first.

"Okay, Jacob, take it easy," someone said, the voice low and soothing. "You're coming out from under the meds, and it's going to be a little disorienting. But you're in the hospital, and you're safe."

I didn't recognize the voice, which scared me, and the beeping sound accelerated.

"The noise you're hearing is the heart monitor. Can you open your eyes?" he, the voice, asked, and I realized belatedly that it was dark around me.

With an effort that felt like swimming up through lay-ers of mud, I tried to blink.

A sliver of bright light broke through on one side,

and I winced, tears running down the right side of my face. But the left side felt puffy and numb.

I blinked again, managing to keep my eyes . . . my eye open for a few seconds longer. Enough to see my mom, her face chalky white and pinched with worry, holding my hand. Sarah was perched on the plastic-looking recliner with her, watching warily, with Patsie, her worn stuffed dog, in her lap.

"Hi, baby," Mom said, tears filling her eyes and rolling down her cheeks. She squeezed my right hand carefully, avoiding the IV needle stuck in the back of it.

My dad was at the foot of the bed, his reading glasses pushed up and lost or forgotten in his rumpled dark hair. He touched my foot, but hesitantly, as if it might break. "Welcome back, Jacob." His voice was thick, almost foreign sounding, and he looked away almost immediately.

"What . . ." But making that small sound felt like swallowing razor blades with the sharp edges up, and my eyes watered more fiercely at the pain.

My mom clucked at me in distress. "You shouldn't try to talk." She held a small plastic cup with a straw to my mouth, and I took a cautious sip, the water offering a passing moment of cold relief in my throat. "They just took the breathing tube out this morning. And you're still on oxygen."

Breathing tube. "What . . . happened?" I could feel the

scrape of plastic in my nose and see the flaps of tape on my cheek, probably where the oxygen line was attached.

"Do you remember the accident?" my mom asked, squeezing my hand tighter.

At first, I couldn't remember anything but the darkness, a pitch-black nothingness from which I'd emerged. But then pieces came back slowly, then fell into place.

"Eli. The Jeep. He came to get me." It was like remembering a dream from years ago. "The bridge."

I struggled to sit up, only to find that the entire left side of my body wouldn't move.

"Easy," the unknown voice said to my left, out of my range of sight. "We've spent a lot of time putting you back together."

With effort and a growing weight of dread in my stomach, I turned my head carefully.

A man in scrubs and a white coat was on the left side of my bed, scrawling notes in a chart. But that wasn't the worst part.

My left arm was four times its normal size with bandages, and now that I was looking at it, I could feel the throbbing and sizzle of nerves that felt frayed. And my left leg, beneath the blankets, appeared to be equally swollen and lumpy with bandages.

He set the clipboard down on my bed and flipped a penlight on to shine in my eye, peeling back an eyelid that wouldn't respond to my commands. "Your left eye is swollen shut, but as soon as the inflammation goes down, your sight should be fine. Dr. Sheffield, the neurologist, will be down a little later."

"My arm," I managed.

The doctor turned off the penlight and retrieved his clipboard. "Open fracture of the olecranon process. We've set it surgically." He shrugged, seemingly unconcerned. "With rehab and time, you'll have eighty to ninety percent of normal motion back."

That's not enough, a panicked voice shouted in my head.

But I had to ask. "Baseball?"

"Sure, someday," he said, already lost in whatever notes he was writing down.

My dad cleared his throat. "Jacob is left-handed. He is . . . he was a pitcher."

The doctor hesitated, which told me everything I didn't want to know. "I think you should concentrate on healing for now."

Nausea swirled over me like fog, and I dropped my head back on the pillows. No more pitching? No more baseball? Not ever?

The doctor frowned down at me, as if I'd insulted him. "You weren't wearing a seat belt. You're incredibly lucky to be alive, young man." Then, as if he feared that wasn't enough to impress me, he pointed his pen at me. "You died en route to the hospital. More than once. Took a few tries to keep your heart going. You're lucky someone found you when they did."

I died? The bed seemed to tilt under me like I was falling, though I knew I was lying down.

"It's a miracle," my mom said, trying to smile through her tears. "God was watching over you."

I tried to remember. Dying seemed like it should be one of those things that stuck with you. But between now and the accident—seeing Eli spin away from me—all I had was that inky, suffocating blackness. More than a blank space in my memory, it felt like a complete absence of everything.

What was that? Where was I when that was happening? Was I just gone?

That wasn't supposed to be the way it worked. Eli had given me crap about telling Sarah about the bright light and heaven, but wasn't that the way it was supposed to go? Or something close? Not just . . . nothing.

I could feel cold welling up in me, like my heart was suddenly pumping the icy water from the creek we'd crashed into.

But before I had time to fully process what any of that meant, the doctor's final words jostled for my attention.

You're lucky someone found you when they did. Someone had to find me? But that didn't make any sense. Eli was right there and wearing his seat belt, like a good, responsible citizen. He should have been able to call 911 and do CPR.

Suddenly, his absence from my room seemed enormous and ominous.

"Where's Eli?" I asked, trying to ignore the flicker of warning in the back of my brain and the tension coiling in my gut.

The atmosphere in the room immediately shifted. My mom sucked in a sharp breath and dropped her gaze to the floor, and my father turned away, scrubbing his hands over his face.

"I'll be back this afternoon," the doctor said quietly to everyone and no one as he left the room.

"Is Eli okay?" I persisted, but neither of my parents would look at me. Even with my dad's back to me, though, I could see his shoulders shaking.

The tilting feeling returned, only this time it was more like the entire planet had dropped, trying to shake me off into space.

Sarah stared at me, pressing her mouth into the top of Patsie's head. I'd never seen her this quiet. Ever. Her eyes were wide above the matted fur, like she was holding back a flood of words.

Or trying not to cry.

My mom straightened in her chair, wiping under her

eyes with her free hand. "They told us it was quick," she said, giving me a tremulous smile. "He wouldn't have known what was happening. Just a bump on the head, and then it would be like drifting off to sleep."

"What?" I heard every word, but it was like they bounced off the surface of my brain, refusing to sink in for processing.

What she was saying was impossible. And yet, I could feel a growing emptiness in my middle, as if someone had rammed one of those telephone poles through my gut, cartoon-style.

Her fingers tightened on mine to the point of pain. "Honey, Elijah didn't make it."

EIGHT WEEKS LATER

CHAPTER FOUR

I WOKE UP BEFORE my alarm would have gone off, if I'd bothered to set it.

Gray predawn light filled my room, sapping everything of color. Not that there was much to see. Small heaps of discarded clothes, a stack of books and papers from school, the metal crutches I theoretically no longer needed leaning against the wall. The row of baseball trophies across the top of my bookshelf gleamed in the faint light like enigmatic hieroglyphs from a secret society I was no longer a part of.

I squinted at the clock through the maze of dull orange prescription bottles on my bedside table. 6:45. My mom would be here any minute.

I'd spent the last two months in a half-conscious haze of exhaustion and pain medication, and the one day I really needed to be asleep, to be so thoroughly out that even the most hard-hearted person would feel guilty waking me—that was the day my body decided to take the initiative and flip my eyes open without my permission.

I braced my weight on my right elbow and heaved myself onto my side, turning away from the door. With the awkward plastic cast on my left leg and the stubborn pain and stiffness in my shattered and twice-repaired elbow, movement was no longer the simple, thoughtless reflex it had once been.

Closing my eyes, I willed myself to go back to sleep. But a light tapping at my door signaled my mother's arrival. "Jace? Honey, are you awake?" she asked softly.

I ignored her. My silence wouldn't stop her, but I couldn't bring myself to respond, either.

The knob turned quietly.

"Jace . . . Jacob, it's time to get up for church." She inched closer, her footsteps soft on the carpet, until she touched my shoulder gently.

"I can't." The idea made the air feel too thick to breathe.

She withdrew her hand swiftly, belatedly realizing I was awake. "You can't stay in here forever, Jacob."

Why not? It had worked well enough so far. Take my pills. Sleep. Wake up. Take more pills. Go back to sleep. Try not to think.

"The doctor cleared you for school tomorrow," she said.

Dread pressed down on me at the reminder. "And I said I would go. That's enough," I said without turning over.

"But the congregation, they've been worried, praying for you," she said. "So many people have been asking after you. They want to see you."

I didn't want to see them, though. And I didn't want them to see me.

If I went today, I'd feel the condemnation in every glance, every whisper, even in the sympathetic smiles.

I wasn't sure I could stand it.

I lurched awkwardly onto my back and turned to face my mom to plead my case. But she looked tired, years older, her face sagging and pale above the bright blue robe that Eli, Sarah, and I had given her for Christmas. Her blond hair, a shade or two darker than ours . . . than mine, appeared washed out and gray.

Worry, fear, and grief were etched in the lines around her eyes and mouth. And I'd put them there.

"It's important to get back into a routine," she said gently.

"Important for who?" I asked. But I already knew. If I went back to school without going to church today, it would be perceived as a "rebellion," even if I didn't mean it to be. There would be talk, some of it behind closed doors and in private phone calls, but some in concerned visits to my dad's office, who'd have to deal with it all. And the pressure would only intensify.

Whether it was difficult for me to step back into a life that was all sharp edges and no soft landing places, a life that no longer felt like mine—that didn't matter.

"Jace, I know this isn't easy . . . ," Mom began.

I ignored her, my attention caught by movement in the hallway behind her. Sarah, in her nightgown, with her reddish curls in a staticky bed head halo, hovered at the edge of the shadows in the doorway, staring at me and clutching her ragged stuffed dog. Patsie's left ear was matted and worn from years of Sarah rubbing it as she fell asleep. Sarah also had the frayed afghan that served as her blankie hoisted over her small shoulder, like she was going into battle against the monsters in the closet. She hadn't carried either of them regularly in a couple of years, but now they were her constant companions.

Mom followed my gaze toward the doorway.

"Sares," I said, my voice creaky with the effort of trying not to scare my sister away.

But like every other time, she bolted soundlessly as soon as I spoke to her. It was like living with a little ghost.

Clearly, I wasn't the only one struggling with my parents' "get back to normal" strategy.

My mother sighed, then turned back to me.

"If we go to early service, it'll be in the sanctuary," she reminded me. "Not the auditorium."

The auditorium, where they held all the largest services, including my brother's funeral. The one I, broken and barely coherent and in the hospital, had not been able to attend.

My mom had offered to show me photos people had taken, but I couldn't look at them. Not yet. Maybe not ever. Seeing Eli, pale and still, laid out in his dark blue suit, surrounded by stands of white lilies—it was too much. So was the weekly visit she made to his grave, one she invited me to make with her every time.

My last memory of Eli was of him alive, and it was burned into my brain.

His face is pale in the dashboard lights, his eyes wide with panic, and his mouth is open as if he's shouting at me. Or for me.

As disturbing as that mental image was, I needed to keep it.

I squeezed my eyes shut.

My mom touched my shoulder, resting her hand there lightly. "Honey, as much as we miss him, we have to remember that Eli is in a better place." She paused. "I'm just glad you were with him at the end, that he wasn't alone."

With her words, the familiar flush of panic returned, and sweat broke out on my skin. Without any help from me, my mom seemed to have latched on to a very specific, comforting idea of what happened that night: Eli and I together at the end of a long dark tunnel, sharing one last hug before he headed into the light and I returned here to resume my life.

Not even close.

I opened my eyes. "Mom, do you think . . . I mean, is Eli . . ." I couldn't find the words, and trying to formulate the question in my head made me want to reach for my pain pills and blot the world out. "How do you know that he's in a better place?" I managed finally.

My mom frowned. "Because that's what we believe."

"But how do you *know*?" I persisted. "How do you know he's not just . . . gone?" My voice broke.

Her breath escaped in a tight gasp. "Because we do, Jacob," she said sharply, but her eyes flooded with tears.

"Mom . . ."

"Please." She stepped back from me, her hands folded and clutched at the center of her chest, like she was applying pressure to a wound.

Guilt flashed through me, lightning fast and hot. She already couldn't handle what had happened. Dumping more on her would be wrong.

"I'm sorry," I said immediately, my eyes burning. "I'm sorry, Mom." Saying it wasn't enough, and repeating it didn't help. It would never be enough.

"It's all right," she said, but she wouldn't look at me.

With an effort, I pushed myself up into a sitting position. "I'll go. Okay?" It was the least I could do, the smallest amends I could make for everything I'd messed up.

She nodded, blinking rapidly, her eyes red and bright with tears. "Thank you." As she turned to leave, she paused, glancing back at me with a strained and trembling smile. "You never know," she said, "it might help, Jacob. Just to be there, to pray."

I doubted that.

But I nodded, because that was what she needed to see. And because some part of me really wanted her to be right.

As it turned out, agreeing to go to church and actually getting there were two different things.

We were late. It was 8:03, and we were hurrying from the overflow parking lot, a block and a half away from the original church. My mom had offered to drop me off, but there was no way I was going in alone. Not today.

"Come on, Sarah," my mom said over her shoulder with an anxious frown, her forehead furrowed with deep wrinkles. She'd already chewed off most of her pale pink lipstick. I'd watched her do it as she searched in vain for a closer place to leave the minivan. "Stop dawdling."

But Sarah, silent and holding tight to Patsie, was only

a step or two behind her, far closer than I was.

I grimaced and put more effort into swinging my left leg forward, my shambling attempt at walking.

I had more metal in me now than the most dedicated body modifier: pins, plates, rods, and screws of all sizes in my elbow and tibia. A freaking hardware store beneath my skin.

The cast on my leg was removable at least, which made it easier to shower, and I'd ditched the splint on my elbow, with my doctor's permission, a couple of weeks ago.

But I was still moving way slower than usual. Doing things right-handed—because the healing bones and torn ligaments in my left arm restricted the use of my left hand—took more time. Brushing my teeth was an ordeal that involved bending my neck to bring my mouth to the toothbrush. And I could only button up about half my shirt without help. There was no question we were late because of me.

"It's fine," my mom said, as much to herself as to Sarah and me. "We'll sneak in the side aisle. Not a problem." She flashed us a reassuring smile that was a little too tight around the edges.

As we rounded the corner and the wooden double doors of the front entrance came into view, my mom reached back and caught Sarah's hand, tugging her forward.

Tension increased in me with every step, and the

orange juice I'd gulped down with my pills burned in my stomach, so much so that it felt like steam might pour out if I opened my mouth.

Like holy water on a vampire.

My mom's heels clicked up the stone stairs, Sarah shuffling her feet to keep up.

You can do this, I told myself. But I didn't sound so sure.

For about the millionth time since the accident, I wished for Eli, wished that he were walking next to me, telling Mom not to worry, saying that everyone was late sometimes. And then quietly urging me to hurry up.

The dull and constant ache in my chest sharpened at the renewed realization that he would never do that again. That I was truly on my own, not only at church, but everywhere. Forever.

As I reached the steps, a bright blue neon sign flickered to life in the front window of the small house across the street, drawing my attention.

Psychic Mary's.

For the first time, I wondered if Mary turned on the sign on Sunday, at church time, deliberately, to signal that she considered herself an equal, a spiritual competitor, and she was open for business too.

"Come on, Jace," my mom called from the top of the stairs, a barely disguised edge of panic in her voice. Her mouth remained fixed in a polite smile, in case anyone was watching.

She tugged at one of the heavy doors, the ornate, twisted metal handle almost as thick as my wrist, but it barely budged.

"Wait," I said, levering myself up the stairs, my progress painful and slow. "I'll help you."

An usher appeared in the small gap my mom had created with her efforts, and pushed the door open the rest of the way, holding it for her and Sarah.

Once they were inside, he moved out onto the landing and stood with his back against the door, keeping it from closing, while he waited for me with a beatific smile.

The familiar smell of church—candle wax, wood polish, and old paper—drifted past him. It was a scent I would know anywhere. Today, it made my heart beat too fast, in anticipation and sickening fear.

"Welcome back, young man," the usher said when I reached the threshold. I probably should have known his name, but I didn't. Eli was always way better at that kind of thing.

"Thanks," I said, taking the bulletin he handed me, my hand shaking. Hopefully he'd think the trembling was part of my injuries.

The cover this week was a simple line drawing in black and white: an outline of Jesus standing up in a boat, his hand extended toward the rising waves that were threatening to swamp the vessel, while the cowering disciples watched in amazement. Their eyes were blank circles, to indicate shock.

To me, they just looked empty.

With effort, I made myself step up and into the narthex, and the usher carefully pulled the door closed after me.

"Jace," my mom whispered.

I blinked, my eyes adjusting to the sudden dimness, and saw her waiting with Sarah and another usher at the right side door to the sanctuary. Through the glass windows, I could see my dad in front of the altar, in his black suit and white clerical collar for the traditional service and with his dark curly hair gelled into TV-ready status for the later services. We'd missed the entire processional and likely the opening prayer.

My mom waved me forward, the urgency clear in her eyes.

There is no "sneaking" anywhere when you're the pastor's family, especially when the pew designated as yours is two from the front.

Avoiding the sight of that pew, one that would still feel empty even once the three of us were sitting in it, I joined my mother and Sarah at the door to the sanctuary. As soon as the usher pulled the door open, my dad's voice, jovial and warm, poured out.

". . . will be meeting at seven o'clock in the library on Tuesday. Refreshments will be provided. Charles Shaw has promised there will be cookies this time. No more fruit-cake leftovers!"

There was an appreciative titter from the congregation.

The timing wasn't going to get any better for us to barge in.

My mom crossed the threshold, from the tile of the narthex to the carpeted sanctuary aisle, her shoulders straight and her smile firmly affixed, guiding Sarah in front of her.

I followed reluctantly.

The sanctuary was an enormous open space, filled with bright light that poured in through stained glass set high in the brick walls. Three columns of dark wooden pews with red velvet cushions lined the room. And on either side of the altar, there were more pews in the transepts.

Banners hung on stands at intervals in both side aisles, including the one we walked down. Most of them were a garish gold and purple for Lent. I'd missed all of Epiphany.

An ornate cross in gold was bolted to the back wall, dominating the space behind the altar.

I couldn't remember a time when I wasn't in this building almost every day. First when my grandpa was pastor, then my dad. We belonged here, even when that belonging felt more claustrophobic than comforting.

But today, the sanctuary felt strangely fake, like a set in the movie of my life. It was a perfect reproduction and yet was missing something essential at the core.

Despair spiraled through me.

The whispers started in the back rows and moved forward as I limped in behind my mom and Sarah.

With every step, it grew harder to breathe. I couldn't hear what they were saying about me, but I could imagine. *His fault. Got his brother killed. Reckless, irresponsible behavior. At a party with drinking!*

"Next week, we'll have an update on our youth mission trip to Guatemala," my dad continued, his smooth patter unfailing, despite the disruption we were causing. "And in two weeks, the senior high youth group will be gathering for pizza and prayer in the auditorium. Please see Kathy or Keith to register."

We were halfway down the aisle when someone close to me at the end of a pew whispered, "God bless you."

I stiffened, almost stumbling in surprise.

It spread from there. "Welcome back." "So good to see you." "We're so sorry about Eli." "We've been praying for you." All voiced in hushed tones so as not to interrupt my dad, who continued to read through the announcements.

At the front of the church, in a pew behind ours, a head turned to stare.

Leah, Eli's girlfriend. Her gaze was fixed on me. She

was pale and visibly trembling, but that wasn't the worst part.

The expression on her face was a mix of wrenching grief, raw pain, and the tiniest portion of terrible hope.

I knew that look. I'd witnessed it on the faces of my family, especially in the first few days after the accident. Eli and I were twins. Seeing me was like seeing Eli, only not. I was an inescapable reminder of what they'd lost, a truckload of salt rubbed into an open and bleeding wound.

As I watched, Leah's eyes rolled back into her head, and she slumped sideways. Her mother caught her, and a murmur rose through the crowd near them.

I swallowed hard, my stomach churning with nausea.

A hand caught at mine, startling me.

I glanced down in surprise. I hadn't even realized I'd stopped moving.

An old woman, in her seventies or maybe eighties, smiled up at me and closed her other hand over mine, clasping it. Her bones were frail beneath that paper-thin skin, the dark blue veins between her knuckles ropy and prominent.

"God saved you for a reason," she said with a knowing wink of her watery blue eyes. "He brought you back for a purpose."

At her words, hot plumes of acid flooded the back of

my throat. I was going to be sick on the floor in the sanctuary if I didn't move.

I tore free from the elderly woman's gentle grasp.
"Sorry," I managed, and headed as fast as I could for the
doors at the back. A wave of gasps followed my retreat.

I made it through the narthex and down the steps
outside, barely, before heaving my orange juice into the
bushes, right below the Riverwoods Bible Church sign.

CHAPTER FIVE

THE RUMBLE OF THE garage door signaled the approach of my fate. It also served as a three-minute warning, sending everyone scrambling to find their places.

"Jace, table, now!" My mom called from downstairs, and by the time I made it to the railing at the top of the stairs that overlooked the lower level, she was already moving into the dining room.

She glanced up at me, her hands full with the serving platter of roast beef. "Grab the potatoes, please." Her thumbs were white on the edge of the plate.

Family dinner on Sunday was a requirement, no matter what else was going on. Baseball, debate team, whatever. Didn't matter.

Even on days when I bolted from church and made a huge scene, apparently. Not that I was the only one. Sarah had flipped out, crying and screaming, as soon as I was out of sight.

When my mom had found me outside, racked by dry heaves, she'd said nothing. Just started for the van, a sobbing Sarah clinging to her legs.

Once we were in the van, heading home, she asked, without looking at me, "It's too much, right? That's all. It's too hard to be there without him." Her voice had broken on the last words, her hand flying up to cover her mouth. She was, I was sure, describing her own feelings as much as mine.

So I'd simply nodded.

I couldn't talk to her, not just about Eli but about what I'd seen—or hadn't—that night when I was . . . gone. The blackness where there should have been light, and the creeping fear of what that meant. And telling my dad? Forget it. He'd probably cite chapter and verse from the Bible, just as Eli would have. And I might be tempted to let him try. Except I didn't want to know how much worse it would feel if he failed to make his case.

I limped downstairs to the kitchen, grabbed the bowl of mashed potatoes off the island counter, and followed my mom's path into the dining room.

The sight of five chairs at the polished wooden table made a bolt of fresh pain go through me, as it always did. My mom and Sarah on one side, me and Eli on the other, with my dad on the end. That's the way it used to be, anyway.

Sometimes, I wished they would rearrange our places and take the extra chair away, instead of leaving it there like a broken tooth that everyone pretended not to see.

Bracing myself, I sat in my chair. Sarah's place was set, but she was, per her now usual behavior, on the floor beneath the table. Patsie sat as guardian in her chair.

I peeked beneath the table to see what she was doing.

She was tucked against the legs of her chair, making two of her My Little Ponies gallop along the bottom rung. Her mouth moved with silent horse noises, hooves clopping, maybe.

"Hey," I whispered. "Are you okay?"

She ignored me, her ponies pausing only for a second before continuing their journey.

I straightened up as my mom returned from the kitchen with a basket of rolls covered in a green cloth napkin that matched the place mats.

Everything looked magazine-perfect, except for us. My mom wore that excess worry in the wrinkles in her forehead, and Sarah was a ghost. And me . . . I didn't want to think about what I looked like in this messed-up diorama of "home."

The steady clip of my dad's wingtips grew louder as he

crossed from the mudroom through the family room to the hall.

I steeled myself for the lecture, his downturned mouth, the carefully measured anger and disappointment in me. Again.

I'd been here more times than I could count—getting in trouble for something I'd done or said. Sunday dinner was always the reckoning.

But my dad just dropped into his chair with a sigh, removing the white plastic collar at his throat.

"Looks great," he said to my mom.

"Great," my mom said back to him with a forced cheeriness.

I watched them both warily. What was this?

"Sarah, do you want to lead us in grace?" my dad asked.

There was no response. Which wasn't a surprise. That was exactly how it had been last week and the week before that and the week before . . .

Without missing a beat, my dad started instead. "Come, Lord Jesus, be our guest and let these gifts to us be blessed. Amen."

The serving spoons clanked against the bowls as my dad served himself and then passed everything to my mom. Like everything was normal, which was the most abnormal response I could think of.

My mom put tiny portions on Sarah's plate, concentrating on cutting her meat and doling out peas on her plate as if they were individually numbered and needed to be in the correct order.

The silence grew thicker and heavier with every second that passed. No one said a thing, not even when Sarah appeared only long enough to grab her plate and take it beneath the table with her.

"Can you pass the butter?" my dad asked, and I jolted at the break in the quiet.

My mom handed him the butter plate and matching knife.

Was no one going to say anything? Really?

"Jace," my mom prompted.

I tensed, my hand tight around my fork.

"Give me your plate." She waved her hand at me in a summoning gesture.

Oh.

I passed it across to her and she loaded my plate as carefully, cutting my meat as she had Sarah's. It was as embarrassing as it was necessary. I could manage a fork right-handed, but a knife and fork would require both hands and my left arm wasn't fully cooperating, especially with anything that required precise movements.

"How were the other services?" my mom asked my dad as she handed me back my plate.

Finally. Now it was coming. I steadied myself in my chair. *Jacob Christopher, what were you thinking?*

"Attendance was up. We had some AV issues, but John said that it was localized to the auditorium, the broadcast should be fine." My dad focused on mixing his peas into his potatoes.

"That's good."

I waited, my breath shallow.

"Jacob," my dad said.

I found I couldn't look at him, not for a long moment. When I managed to, he barely glanced in my direction.

"Can you pass the rolls, please?" he asked.

I passed them over, and he took them without further comment.

That was it?

My spine sagged toward the back of my chair. I should have been relieved. But instead, anxiety bloomed like an impossible itch beneath my skin.

It was a familiar pattern: get caught, get yelled at and/ or punished, and get forgiven.

But now what? What did the non-acknowledgment of my mistakes mean?

I forced myself to pick up my fork and eat a bite of roast.

Maybe this was what happened when you were no longer forgivable, no matter what punishment or penance you were willing to do. We'd never talked about the accident, not after that first day in the hospital.

The quiet clanking of silverware continued, along with my mother's measured questions about church and my dad's short answers.

The weight of everything unspoken pressed down on me from above, until I wished I could hide under the table with Sarah. Part of me wanted to shout, to make them look at me and *see* me. Except I was a little afraid that if I did, they'd just keep passing the food.

I swallowed another dry bite of roast.

No matter how much I'd been dreading going back to school tomorrow, it had to be better than this. Or at least not as awful.

School was secular, away from all my questions and doubts, and away from this house, where everything triggered a memory of Eli. At school, Eli and I had moved in different circles, with different friends.

Maybe tomorrow, for a few minutes, I could escape, even if I didn't deserve to.

CHAPTER SIX

"YOU'RE SURE ABOUT THIS?" my mom asked, for the third time, as she made the final turn into the high school parking lot. It was jammed with cars and people flocking toward the main building.

The sight of them, friends and strangers, laughing, talking, shoving into each other, like everything was normal, simultaneously filled me with relief and made my stomach ache like someone had reached in and hollowed out my guts.

I fought the urge to look over my shoulder to the second seat, where Eli used to sit. He was always a moment too slow in calling shotgun.

"Jacob?"

"It's fine," I said. The truth was, no, I wasn't sure. But maybe focusing on something else like school would help.

I let the silence spin out as further answer because there was nothing else I could say.

"Okay," she said, sounding helpless and resigned. "I'll be here at three to pick you up for PT." She put the van in park, directly across from the main front doors, where everyone was gathering, waiting for the first bell.

I nodded, shoved the door open, and then bent down to pick up my overloaded backpack from the floor with my good arm. Almost two months of assignments, and all of my books for the semester were not light.

"Thanks for the ride, Mom," I said as I half slid, half stepped out of the van and then slammed the door closed.

The van idled in the turnaround for a few more seconds: my mom waiting to see if I'd turn back.

But I didn't. I couldn't go home, not right now.

I limped toward the bike rack to the left of the main doors, where my friends usually waited. It felt like centuries since I'd last been here. The plastic walking cast on my leg made a rough, grating noise on the concrete that I could hear even over the laughter and talking from everybody.

People noticed me right away, some of them moving out of my path. Whether to give me more room to pass or to have a better look, I wasn't sure. A couple nodded hello to me, but most seemed content to stare.

My friends were crowded near the doors, as usual.

Kylie was the first to see me. Her hands flew up to her mouth, the color draining from her face.

"Hey, man, welcome back," Derek managed after a minute.

"We didn't know you were coming today," Matt offered, shifting his weight from foot to foot before stepping up to bump his fist with mine.

When he moved back, an awkward silence reigned. I shouldn't have been surprised. I hadn't responded to any of their texts or called them back since the accident. I didn't know what to say to them, then or now.

Kylie took a big, gulping breath, her eyes watery and her mascara leaving smudges on her cheeks, and I wanted to run. "Are you . . . I mean, is everything . . . ," she tried.

Derek cleared his throat. "So sorry about Eli." The pity in his expression made my skin feel tight, and the urge to run increased.

I only wanted a moment of normal, but I was beginning to realize that normal no longer existed, anywhere.

"Excuse me. Hey, watch out. Coming through." I heard Zach's voice before I saw him, and I turned. The top of his dark red hair bobbed toward us as he cut through the crowd almost as easily as I had.

Zach jerked his chin in greeting when he broke through. "Hey, man, what's up?" he asked with a smile that eased some of the tension in me and everybody else.

I could almost hear my other friends drawing a relieved breath at his arrival.

"I heard you were coming back today," he said. "Why didn't you text me?" Like everything was normal. He was good at that, smoothing things over. Pretty much the opposite of me. We'd been best friends since kindergarten.

"We were waiting for you," Audrey chimed in, trailing after him. Her green eyes went wide as soon as she saw me up close. "Oh, my God, your face."

"Audrey," Zach said sharply.

"I . . . I'm sorry," she faltered. "I didn't know." Then she turned to Zach. "You said it was just his leg and his elbow," she hissed at him.

Behind me, I could sense Kylie and the others shifting, uncomfortable.

"It is, mostly," I answered for Zach. "The scar will fade." That's what the various medical professionals kept telling me. If not, they said there was always plastic surgery. I'd been lucky to come away with only one long gash from the top of my left temple down past my cheekbone. The majority of the windshield had splintered and broken away before I went through it.

Honestly, most of the time I forgot about the reddish-purple mark, when I wasn't looking in the mirror, which I did as little as possible.

Zach and Audrey nodded, almost in unison, their hands interlaced tightly between them.

"Did your mom tell you I stopped by last week?" Zach asked, stuffing his free hand deep in the pocket of his letterman's jacket. I had an almost identical one hanging in my closet at home.

"Yeah, sorry, I didn't feel up to talking."

"Kind of picked up on that," he said. Audrey elbowed him, and he grunted as the air escaped his lungs. "Sorry," he added. "I just wanted to make sure you were okay. After I came over that one time, it seemed . . ."

Messed up. Heavy. Depressing. Awful. Any one of those words could apply. Zach had brought over all my books and assignments the week I got home from the hospital. That was before my parents had implemented their "act normal" strategy. So, at that point, my dad was basically living at the church office, burying himself in work; my mom was prone to crying silently outside Eli's door; my sister was mid-transformation to silent ghost; and I was a zombie, drugged up on pain meds, foggy and struggling to get a grip on what I'd caused.

It wasn't a whole lot better now, honestly.

"I wanted to come back, but your mom said I should wait until you were better. And you never texted me back . . ." Zach trailed off helplessly, running out of words.

"It's okay," I said. "Not your fault. I was trying to figure out some stuff." Which was a lie. Made it sound like I'd actually gotten somewhere in the last few weeks. But maybe it was better to pretend. Maybe Mom and Dad were onto something.

Zach bobbed his head in acknowledgment, his shoulders losing tension and dropping to a more normal position.

But I sensed there was more, from the look he and Audrey exchanged with each other.

"About that night—" Zach began.

"—we're so sorry," Audrey put in. "If we hadn't gotten in that stupid fight—"

"You were counting on me to be DD, man, and I shouldn't have—" Zach continued.

"It's all right," I said. I didn't want them to go over it all again—didn't need them to. I'd done it a thousand times or more in my head. It wasn't their fault. It was mine.

The awkward silence returned for a long moment. Matt, Kylie, and the others behind me started a separate quiet conversation. And everyone else around us had gone back to whatever they were doing, but some of the closer ones were listening.

My gaze caught on a girl standing with a cluster of her friends. She was the only one facing me, and her cheeks were wet with tears that had cut tracks in her makeup. Her eyes were red-rimmed and swollen behind her thick-framed glasses. Her sweatshirt said BIG TALK, BIG WALK in huge letters. Debate team.

I looked away from the girl.

"So, uh, let me see your schedule," Zach said with forced cheer, drawing my attention to him. "I don't know where you're at this semester."

Silently, I dug into my pocket for the crumpled sheet of paper and then handed it over.

Zach released Audrey's hand to take the page and unfolded it. "Government first hour? That blows."

Audrey made a sympathetic noise, her anxious gaze bouncing between my face and Zach's.

"But I heard Mr. Peterson will give you extra credit if you—" Zach stopped and frowned at the paper. "Whoa, wait a minute. They messed this up. They took you out of lifting and put you in Pussy PE." He looked up at me, confused.

Varsity athletes took weight lifting and training, so we could stay in shape in the off-season. No pathetic pickle ball, badminton, or bowling for us. "Pussy PE" is what everyone called the study hall for kids who were too messed up to handle even regular gym.

In other words, me now.

"Zach," Audrey said through her teeth in protest. But it had no effect. He was staring at me, waiting for an answer.

"I can barely walk, dude," I pointed out, trying to clamp down on my frustration at being forced to discuss the obvious. "Running and lifting are kind of out of my reach."

I'd wanted to fight that change in my schedule, but what was I going to do? Sit on the bleachers for the next three months? Plus, I'd been overruled by my mom and Mrs. Schultz, the guidance counselor, who both thought the additional study time would be more valuable in helping me catch up so I could graduate on time.

"Yeah, but Coach is going to be pissed if you're not in shape for the season." He paused, and I saw it click for him for the first time. His eyes widened. "You're not . . . wait, are you out for good?" He sounded horrified.

Yes, I was. Left-handed pitchers are prized beyond all measure, but once you shatter your elbow, you're damaged goods, a ticking time bomb waiting to land on the disabled list at the worst possible moment. No serious college team is going to take that chance, not when there are so many other players competing for the same spot. Coach and I had already had this conversation, when he'd come by the house a couple of weeks ago.

"I don't know. Maybe. It depends," I hedged. I couldn't take his reaction to the truth.

The shock on Zach's face told me he'd never considered the possibility. Obviously Coach hadn't made the announcement to the whole team yet.

"It's okay," I said again, feeling like that was all I could say these days. But it was always a lie.

Zach blinked at me, stunned into silence.

"Um, hi," a new voice said, startling all of us.

The girl in the debate team sweatshirt had left her friends to hover near me, her hands tucked up inside her sleeves.

"I wanted to say, I'm so sorry about Eli." Her voice cracked, and fresh tears rolled down her cheeks. "He was on the debate team with me, with us." She gestured to her group of friends, who were now watching with damp-eyed gazes. "He was, like, really, really good."

Zach and Audrey exchanged uncomfortable looks.

It took a second for my drilled-in manners to kick in. "Thanks," I said, forcing a smile that felt more like baring my teeth.

"And he was so nice," she continued, choking on a sob. "When we went to Springfield last year for tournament, I forgot to bring extra money for food. And I couldn't tell Mrs. Springer because she would have flipped out. But Eli . . ." She paused, her lower lip trembling. "He bought me cheeseburgers. Like every day for three days. He knew they were my favorite somehow." She laughed through her tears. Then her face crumpled, and she was crying for real.

Oh, no.

I looked helplessly to Audrey and Zach for an assist, but they were both studying the ground like it held the answers to the next SAT prep test.

"Yeah," I said finally. "Eli was like that." And he was, always paying attention to everybody else around him, collecting details, trying to make people happy. Perfectly perfect, leaving me to be perfectly inadequate, which had been fine when he was here. But now what?

Not knowing what else to say, I reached out and patted the debate team girl's shoulder. It seemed like an Eli thing to do.

But my action only seemed to encourage her grief. She crashed into me, throwing her arms around me like I was the only piece of solid land for miles.

Anyone who'd stopped staring previously had now rejoined the fun, as I tried to keep my balance.

"I keep telling myself that it's okay, that he's, like, in a better place, right?" She looked up at me, desperation and misery written across her face. She wanted me to reassure her, to help her, even though I had no idea who she was.

It clicked then with a jolt that I felt through my whole body: I was her Eli stand-in. As difficult as it was for my family, Leah, and probably others to look at me and see Eli, this girl was the opposite. She was looking for me to *be* him, to say what he would have said.

"Right. Yes." The words tasted like lies, but I forced

them out anyway. What was I supposed to do instead? Shove her off me and tell her I had no idea? That I got Eli killed and the darkness I'd experienced might mean there was no "better place"?

She nodded, and I could feel her trembling recede slightly.

The bell rang then, way too late to save me, and she released me, backing away with an embarrassed smile. "Thank you," she said with a deep breath and a few remaining sniffles.

"Sure." The tension in my jaw and neck tightened until it seemed like something in there might snap.

"You okay, man?" Zach asked uncertainly.

No. "Yeah. Let's get out of here," I said, limping toward the doors.

The morning went downhill from there. In the back of my mind, I must have thought that the worst was over, but nope.

By the time I got to fourth hour, Pussy PE, my face hurt from maintaining a semblance of a polite smile, and my skin felt thin from too many people touching me, whether it was a reassuring thump on the back or more full-on, sneak-attack hugs that were an attempt to console or meant to be a sign of mutual grief. And the longer I was here, the more comfortable people seemed to be with approaching me.

I couldn't deal. My pain meds were wearing off, and the nurse's office seemed like an impossibly long hobble away from this end of the building.

Pussy PE was held in one of the smaller chemistry labs not in use this hour. I paused at the doorway to look for a place to sit and to catch my breath. Hauling myself up and down the hallways with the cast, as light as it was, was work. Even with physical therapy twice a week, I wasn't prepared.

Most of the seats were already filled. I recognized a few faces, mostly from the mocking they took when they showed up on the first day of gym with their schedule change to be initialed by Coach or Mrs. Lloyd.

A girl in a wheelchair with a cannula running from her nose sat next to a chick in a back brace. Then there was a dude who appeared to have something wrong with his hands; they were too thin and curved in oddly toward his chest. Another kid had no fewer than three asthma inhalers laid out precisely on the table in front of him, like surgical instruments.

It was a room full of broken and damaged people. The dent-and-scratch section of the school, like the aisle of the appliance store where my parents used to get all of our refrigerators, washers, and dryers before they had the money to buy better.

And I was now one of them.

With a barely repressed sigh, I limped into the room.

Everyone stared, but by this point, I was too tired to care. The only empty seat was next to Chad Hardwick—a tall, superskinny guy rumored to have hemophilia—in the third row on the left side.

As I approached, a girl in the second row glanced up at me, shoving her dark and crazy curly hair out of her face. Then she froze, her mouth open.

Surprised recognition pinged through me. *Thera Catoulus.*

Of course she'd be in here. Last year, she'd claimed that Doug and Aaron had cornered her in the gym on their way from the lifting room. The principal probably didn't want to give her an opportunity to make more accusations of harassment. Putting her in Pussy PE would keep her under closer supervision and out of the way.

Thera's face, already so white that her eyebrows were like dark slashes, paled further, and her throat worked in a hard swallow as she stared at me. She half rose from her seat and then stopped, confusion and a horrible flash of hope crossing her face.

Oh, shit. She thought I was Eli.

Eli had always collected people; I'd just never realized how many until today. I'd never realized Thera was among them, either. My dad would have been pissed if he knew.

As kids, that had been one of the earliest warnings Eli

and I had been given at the church: stay away from across the street. My parents hadn't even called it Psychic Mary's, probably for fear that we'd be more interested. Her services were, according to my dad, "not something you want to mess with," and then there was what it would've looked like if we were caught over there. Even in the yard.

I waited with dread for the burst of tears when Thera realized who I was. Or rather, who I wasn't. It had been happening off and on all day.

But instead, the moment it clicked, Thera recoiled, jerking back as if she'd smelled something bad, her lip curling in disgust as she dropped into her seat.

Whatever. I kept moving toward the third row. I needed to sit down before I fell down.

"Hey, man," I said to Chad. "This seat taken?"

He shook his head, but scooted over to the far edge of the table, as if I might shove him there anyway.

I dropped into the plastic chair, shrugged my backpack off to the floor, where it landed with a resounding thud, and stretched my leg out in front of me, swallowing a groan of relief.

Ahead of me, Thera had frozen in a rigid posture, her shoulders squared as though I might chuck a book or a throwing star or something at her from behind.

"Greetings, children," Mr. Sloane said with a wave of his coffee mug, his MacBook tucked under his arm. He was the drama teacher and had been supposedly working on a screenplay on the side for, like, the last ten years.

He nodded at me, an acknowledgment of my addition to the class, and then moved a red-and-blue molecular model of something out of the way and set down his laptop. Within seconds, he was engrossed in whatever was on his screen.

The hour passed slowly, each minute ticking loudly on the ancient analog clock that hung crookedly on the opposite wall.

It was so quiet I could hear the asthmatic kid breathing, and so hot I could feel sweat trickling down my spine. I didn't belong here.

After a while, the words on the page in front of me— *The Great Gatsby* for English—began to blur together. With only a few minutes left in the period—how was I going to get through this every day?—I gave up and leaned back in my chair to massage the overworked muscles in my right leg. My gaze landed on Thera. She was practically invisible behind her long hair, her head down as she scrawled in her notebook.

When the bell rang, she jolted at the sound and stood quickly to stuff her notebook and books into a ragged canvas bag covered with a weird mix of patches, including some I recognized from a brief stint in the Boy Scouts.

She was tall, probably only a few inches shorter than me. I'd never been close enough to her before to notice. Her clompy black combat boots and tight dark jeans, almost as black as her hoodie and her hair, made her look even taller. The jeans also drew attention to a rather spectacular ass, which I felt vaguely guilty for noticing.

When she slammed the last book in place, a pen fell out and skittered across the floor.

I spoke up without thinking. "Hey, you lost your—"

She spun around, and to my shock, her dark eyes were filled with tears. Then she leaned toward me until mere inches separated us. I could see one tiny freckle, like a spot of ink, under her right eye.

"It should have been you," she said, each word a cold, hard bullet, enunciated carefully so I wouldn't miss it. "Eli was worth ten of you."

Her words stole my breath. It was something I'd been thinking, something I knew other people thought. No one else had had the balls to say it.

But it was the raw grief in her eyes, as deep, horrible, and personal as anything I'd seen from Leah yesterday, that really shook me. I'd been watching people cry over Eli all day. Eli as a concept. Eli as the nice guy in class. Eli as someone they knew who was now dead.

But this was different. Who was this girl to Eli? Or maybe, who had Eli been to her?

She straightened up abruptly and turned away, moving toward the door with purpose.

"Hey, wait," I called after her.

But she ignored me.

By the time I levered myself to my feet and limped to the door, she was halfway down the hall, threading her way through the mob. As I watched, she gathered her hair and tucked it into the neck of her shirt with a practiced motion. Then she tugged her hood up and over her head and vanished into the crowd, like a magic trick.

CHAPTER SEVEN

THE ONLY GOOD THINGS about physical therapy were that it was exhausting and it hurt. Getting through the reps and exercises took everything I had, to the point where I couldn't focus on anything but getting through it.

And then afterward, I was normally too tired to think about anything except the pain and trembling sense of overwork in my arm and leg.

But not today, unfortunately.

My brain kept cycling back to Thera Catoulus. What she'd said. How she'd stormed off.

Her reaction didn't seem like everyone else's. That wasn't just grief today. That was anger and frustration and loss, and you didn't feel that for someone who, I don't know, loaned you a quarter for the vending machine, did you?

Not unless you were seriously unstable, which, okay, maybe she was, given her history.

But she didn't seem unstable. She seemed pissed. A sentiment I completely understood. Which, to me, meant she'd known Eli in a way that would have generated those emotions.

That last night, before we crashed, I'd asked Eli if he was cheating on Leah. He'd been acting so weird. But I'd been joking. Mostly.

Now I wasn't so sure. If he was messing around with Psychic Mary's daughter, that would explain the weird. In more ways than one.

A familiar pang of guilt shot through me. By all logic and justice, he should have been the one to survive. He was the good one. He was the one wearing his seat belt. He was the one who should be here, not the one who was gone.

"Everything all right?" my mom asked, startling me. We were almost home. "Was therapy okay?"

"It was fine." I'd said the same thing about school, when she'd asked.

She sighed, but said nothing more.

Frustration bloomed white-hot. I couldn't give her the detailed reassurances she wanted. I didn't have them to give, not without asking questions about faith, God, and fate that she wouldn't want to hear.

I slunk lower in my seat and kept my head down in an attempt to prevent further inquiries.

The umbrella—pink-and-white-striped—stuffed in the organizational bin between our seats brought back the memory of that bright blue umbrella sailing past my face during the accident.

That night, Eli had been asking questions about doing the right thing. And no matter what he'd said then, I was beginning to think now he hadn't been talking in the theoretical.

"Mom, was everything okay with Eli before . . . before?" I asked. "Do you know if something was bothering him?"

She tensed, glancing over her shoulder to the rear seat, where Sarah was strapped in. When I looked back, Sarah was watching both of us from her booster seat.

"No," Mom said quickly. "Everything was fine." Her tone indicated that this should be the end of the conversation.

I wasn't sure if she was afraid I was trying to question things that were a certainty to her, or if she knew something and didn't want to discuss it.

"But I think maybe he—" I began.

"Jace," my mom said in warning. "Not now."

"Right," I said, swallowing my frustration.

As we rounded the corner onto our street, my mom slowed, frowning.

I followed her gaze. A vaguely familiar SUV, a black BMW, was parked in our driveway.

"Who is that?" I asked. Drop-bys were a big no-no at our house. It was a rule—or it used to be, at least—that all visits had to be cleared ahead of time. The illusion of perfection had to be maintained. No dirty dishes on the counter or piles of laundry spilling out into the hall. Nothing that could be reported back to the congregation or whispered about.

Before she could answer, the front doors of the SUV popped open. On the driver's side, Mr. Hauer, Riverwoods' council president, climbed out. On the other, his daughter and Eli's girlfriend, Leah.

Her long blondish-brown hair swung in a ruthlessly straight line at her shoulders. She was wearing her St. Luke's uniform; the white blouse was slightly rumpled after a long day of classes, but her tie—in the same blue-and-black plaid as her skirt—was perfectly knotted and in place at her throat. She looked washed out, a faded version of herself.

Leah and her dad moved to the back of their SUV to wait for us.

"Can we pretend we don't see them?" I asked my mom. Maybe it made me a coward, but I couldn't do this right now. I couldn't see the pain on her face again.

"Hush," my mom said, but not with any harshness.

My mom pulled in the driveway and parked next to them, summoning a bright smile. "Rick, how wonderful to see you!" she called out as she pushed open her door.

I took an extra second to steel myself and then followed her example.

"Mr. Hauer," I said when I reached them, offering my right hand to the closest thing my dad had to an earthly boss, all too aware of my sweaty clothes and likely stench.

He shook my hand without hesitation, squeezing hard in that man-test kind of way. "Jacob, glad to see you up and about," he said too heartily, as if yesterday had never happened.

Leah said nothing, staring somewhere over my right shoulder, like she couldn't look directly at me.

We stood there for a long awkward beat until my mom intervened.

"Would you like to come in?" she asked. "Let me just get Sarah." She moved past me, squeezing between our vehicle and theirs to pull the sliding side door open.

Before the accident, Sarah would have gotten herself unbuckled and wrestled the minivan door open on her own, or would have at least been loudly protesting about being forgotten.

This version of Sarah was waiting meekly in her seat.

"We don't want to interrupt your afternoon," Mr. Hauer

said as my mom lifted Sarah out and then took her hand. "I'm sure you folks are busy."

Why did everything he said sound so patronizingly jovial and fake? Had it always and I just never noticed?

"Leah wanted a chance to speak with Jacob."

"Of course. Let's go inside." My mom led everyone up the front stairs and through the door, which we never used ourselves, and then turned to me. "Jacob, why don't you and Leah talk in the living room?"

She gestured to the room across from us, as if neither Leah nor I knew where it was located. As if I wanted to have this conversation, whatever it turned out to be, with Leah in any location.

Then my mom turned her attention to Mr. Hauer. "Rick, I have some of that coffee you like. Sumatra, right?"

He nodded. "Yes, that's it." He sounded delighted and surprised. But my mom was good with people.

"Come on back to the kitchen," she said, waving him forward. "Let me get Sarah settled with a snack, and then you can tell me more about the expansion plans. Micah said the council was meeting with the architect again."

With a warning look at me that I couldn't interpret, my mom led Mr. Hauer down the hall, leaving Leah and me alone.

Before I could figure out what to say, Leah turned

on her heel, her plaid skirt flaring out behind her, and headed into the living room.

She sat on the couch. I lowered myself into the armchair across from her, keeping half the room and part of the piano between us.

The uncomfortable silence continued, and I could hear the low murmurs of my mom and Mr. Hauer talking in the kitchen, most likely about us.

"What's up, Leah?" I asked, a little more abruptly than I meant to.

She flinched and then held her hand up in apology. "I forgot how much you two sound alike." She took a deep breath. "And I'm trying to get used to the idea that I'll never hear Eli say my name again." Her eyes went shiny with tears.

I clamped my mouth shut. What could I say to that?

Leah took another breath, then lifted her gaze to meet mine. "I came here because I wanted to say I'm sorry for yesterday."

"Yesterday? For what?"

She sat up straighter, smoothing her hands over her skirt. "That couldn't have been easy for you, coming back to church for the first time since . . ." Her voice faltered. "I didn't mean to make it harder. I haven't been sleeping well."

Was she actually apologizing for fainting? Like that

was something she could control. "It's fine. You have nothing to be sorry for," I said.

"No, I'm not the only one who lost. I need to remember that."

The back of my brain registered the faintly martyred tone in her voice, exactly the kind of thing that made her so irritating, but I was more preoccupied with a larger revelation.

"You're not mad at me," I said, but my surprise made it come out more like a question. After all, maybe she was better at hiding her anger than others.

She shook her head and stared down at her hands folded neatly in her lap. "Of course not."

"Why not?" I blurted. It was an accident, yeah, but the circumstances leading up to it had been put in motion by me.

"Jesus said to forgive seventy times seven, Jace," she said with an admonishing look.

Thanks, Leah, how incredibly helpful. I knew the Bible verse—Matthew something—just as well as she did. Okay, maybe not quite as well. But regardless, what the verse lacked was the *how*. How do you forgive someone that much? How do you forgive yourself? How do you stop being angry? Where was *that* quote?

"Because Jesus told me to" wasn't a particularly compelling or useful explanation in this situation.

Her shoulders sagged. "Besides, it's what Eli would have wanted," she added softly.

I cleared my throat. "Thanks." She was right; Eli probably would have wanted that. But that didn't mean I deserved her forgiveness. Or his, if he were able to give it.

"I also wanted to ask a favor," Leah said. "You knew Eli probably better than anyone besides me."

Maybe. Today of all days, I wasn't so sure about that.

"Would it be weird if we talked about him sometimes?" Her throat worked. "I loved him, and I miss him." Tears rolled down her cheeks to her jaw. "And I thought maybe since you did too, we could . . . I don't know . . ."

Leah had planned her entire future around my brother. They'd spent days comparing course catalogs and college brochures and being generally annoying downstairs in the rec room, while I was playing Xbox. If anyone could have made a relationship in high school survive all the way through college and beyond, it would have been the two of them.

But now here she was, half of a whole that no longer existed. Maybe in that, Leah and I finally had something in common.

"Yeah," I said, rubbing my palms down the legs of my pants. "Whenever you want."

Leah nodded her thanks, wiping under her eyes carefully. After a beat of silence, she started to get up.

A stupid impulse took hold of me. "Wait. Can I ask you something?"

She sank back onto the couch.

I hesitated. The last thing I wanted to do was make her cry more. "Was everything okay with Eli that last night? He, uh, seemed upset about something."

She blinked, confused. "No, I don't . . . I didn't really talk to him much that day. Did something happen at the party?"

I stared at her. "What?"

"It's just, that was more your scene than his." She lifted her shoulders in an uncertain shrug. "Maybe someone said something—"

"At Zach's party," I said slowly, trying to fit the pieces together.

"Yes, Zach's party," she said, giving me a sidelong look. "Eli wanted to spend time with you. What other party was there that night?"

"I . . . none, I guess," I managed, my hand clutching tight to the arm of the chair.

Leah shifted closer to the edge of the cushion, looking at me and my death grip with concern. "Are you okay? Do you need me to get your mom?"

"No," I said too quickly. "I just didn't know that he'd told you that. About wanting to spend time with me, I mean."

Her eyes spilled over again, a sad smile pulling at her mouth. "He told me everything."

No, no, he didn't.

Because Eli sure as hell had not been at Zach's party.

He'd told my parents and me that he was with Leah. And he'd told Leah he was with me.

The realization led to a strange twisting sensation in me, like something long held was breaking loose. *Eli had been lying to all of us.*

But why?

In a flash, I saw again the deep, unmistakable grief on Thera's face.

CHAPTER EIGHT

WHEN I WALKED INTO Pussy PE on Tuesday, Thera was already there, her attention fixed on a thick textbook in front of her and her barely-a-stub pencil scratching across her notebook page. Her dark hair had slid forward over her shoulder, hiding most of her face.

I paused just over the threshold.

Was this really such a good idea? So what if she and Eli were a thing—what difference did it make now?

None.

Except I needed to know. It was like discovering some secret side to Eli, one that was less than perfect and more like me.

Thera didn't look up when I stopped in front of her table, not even when I cleared my throat.

"Hey," I said.

She glanced up, her mouth tightening at the sight of me. "Oh. Hey."

"Can I talk to you?" I asked, and everyone else in the room went still, like we were the featured entertainment. *Damn it.*

She nodded slowly, running her thumbnail over the metal ridges of the eraser end of her pencil. "Listen, if this is about yesterday, I . . . I'm sorry." Her words sounded stilted and forced. "That was a shitty thing to say to you and I'm not—"

"No," I said. "It's not about that." I didn't want an apology from her. That felt wrong. She was the only one who'd had the guts to call it like she saw it.

"Then what?" she asked, her expression radiating wariness.

"My brother," I said, hitching my backpack higher on my shoulder, the motion awkward with my right hand.

Thera went still. "Okay," she said after a moment, pushing away her textbook—physics, I could see now—and putting her pencil down.

"Did he . . . were you . . ." I struggled to find the right words. "What was he to you?" I asked finally. "I saw you yesterday," I added before she could say anything. "You thought I was him."

Her shoulders stiffened. "You're twins," she pointed out, focusing on some undefined spot to my left. "It was a mistake. I forgot for a second. That's all." Then she grabbed her pencil and slid her textbook closer, signaling that the conversation was over.

"I'm just trying to understand," I said quietly. Him, the situation, life, death, everything. It felt like I needed to start somewhere, and this, at least, I could investigate.

Thera didn't respond except to flip a page.

With a wince, I lowered myself carefully to be level with her. "My brother was lying to his girlfriend and everybody else about where he was right before the accident," I said in a voice barely above a whisper.

Her gaze shot to me immediately and then away, color rising in her pale face.

"And you . . . you're . . ." My words failed me again, and when she looked up at me, I could feel the embarrassed flush in my cheeks.

"I'm what?" she asked, in a careful, too neutral tone. "I'm . . . me? Is that what you were going to say? I'm the girl you don't take home to Mom and Dad, just the one you screw in secret and then lie about?"

Oh, shit. "No, that's not what I—"

"You can go now," Thera said.

"Wait, no, that's not it!" I hoisted myself back upright, gritting my teeth against the pull of pain in my leg. "I'm trying to figure out what Eli was doing that night—"

"And you automatically assume he was sleeping with

me?" Thera folded her arms across her chest.

Someone in the back of the room tittered.

"I'm not . . . I didn't . . . ," I protested. How did this spin so out of control, and so quickly? My argument was crumbling fast around me. "You were really upset yesterday. And I just . . . why else would he lie?"

Her expression darkened. "Of course. Because I'm Thera Catoulus and I'll fuck anything that moves, right? Whether they have girlfriends or not. Whether I want to or not." Her voice wavered a little on that last part.

I opened my mouth and shut it, not knowing what to say. A yawning chasm was opening up in what I'd thought was solid ground.

She leaned forward, her dark eyes bright with tears and anger. "Why can't you leave me alone?"

"That's not—"

"Is it because you think I'm poor and desperate, so I'll let you?" she asked. "Or maybe it's because my mom tells fortunes, and lies about talking to dead people, so guys like you can say whatever you want about me and no one will stop you."

Lies about talking to dead people. Her words bounced around in my head, echoing, so it took me a second to process the rest of what she'd said.

"I'm not trying to say anything about you at all," I said, frustrated. "I'm just asking a question." And she was literally the only person in the world who could answer it.

Thera shoved her chair back to stand. "No, you're not!" she shouted.

"Hey, hey! What's going on here?" Mr. Sloane asked as he walked into the room.

"Nothing," Thera said, dropping back into her chair.

"A misunderstanding," I said.

Mr. Sloane sighed. "Thera, go to the office, please."

"What? I didn't do anything. Ask anyone."

A deafening silence followed. No one was going to back her up.

Her shoulders slumped. "Forget it," she muttered, gathering up her belongings.

But her hands were shaking as she shuffled her books and that pathetic excuse for a pencil into her worn bag, and something like guilt moved in me.

"She's right. I started it," I said before I could think better of it.

Thera's fingers slipped off the zipper of her bag as she glared at me.

Mr. Sloane threw his hand up in exasperation. "Fine, both of you go." He frowned at us. "I'll call to make sure you get there. You have three minutes."

Thera stood, swung her bag over her shoulder without comment, and then hauled ass out the door.

• • •

In the hall ahead of me, Thera was a distant figure in all black, her hood up and her head down.

I followed her path to the office, but I couldn't keep up. And I had a feeling that asking her to wait wouldn't get me very far. I wasn't completely sure why I'd said anything. Getting sent to the principal's office automatically meant a call home, and right now, that couldn't be good for me. Either they'd be pissed, which would be bad, or, worse, they'd say nothing at all.

I concentrated on moving one foot in front of the other, trying to move faster.

At the sound of laughter, I looked up.

Caleb had come from somewhere, one of the classrooms probably, and was now walking backward alongside Thera, a bright green hall pass between his fingers.

As I watched, he laughed again and reached out to tug her hood back, touching her hair.

Twisting away from him, she slapped his hand down with a loud smack and walked faster. I couldn't see her face, but she seemed smaller, shrunken somehow. The whole scenario screamed *WRONG*. It made my insides feel squeezed by an invisible fist.

"Hey, Caleb," I called.

He caught sight of me, whispered something to Thera that made her flinch, and then loped toward me.

"Palmer! What's up, man?" Caleb asked with a grin. "What are you doing out here?"

"Office. What are you doing?"

"Library." He flicked the pass and grinned. "Gotta do 'research' on some Shakespeare thing." He squinted at me. "You get in trouble? With her?" He jerked his head in the direction Thera had taken.

I shrugged, uncomfortable. "Something like that."

"Nice." He held his fist out.

"I better go, before Drizen comes looking for me." I moved past him.

"You don't have to chase that hard after her, Palmer," Caleb called after me. "She wants you to catch her."

"Shut up," I mumbled, and he laughed.

When I finally made it to the office and pulled open the door, I was sweaty and exhausted.

"No, he's here now," Mrs. Clark, one of the secretaries, said into the phone as I collapsed in the chair next to Thera's, trying to catch my breath and ignore the fresh throbbing in my leg.

When Mrs. Clark hung up the phone and returned to her computer, Thera skated a glance in my direction, hugging her bag tighter to her body. "I don't need your help," she whispered.

"I never said you did." Though after what I'd seen

in the hallway, I wasn't so sure about that. "I just want answers."

"I don't *have* any answers," she hissed, shifting away from me in her chair. "I told you."

We sat in silence for a few long moments while I tried to figure out how to ask what I needed to know. I had no idea what I could say that wouldn't make things worse.

He was worth ten of you. That's what Thera had said yesterday. And she was right, no matter what reason she had for feeling that way. On that, at least, we were in agreement.

"If you're angry at me for getting Eli killed, you should be," I said finally. "He's the one who should be here, not me."

She stiffened and then looked over at me, her eyebrows raised in surprise.

I shifted my plastic-booted foot on the worn gray carpeting, stretching my leg out and rubbing the muscles around my knee, trying for some relief.

Thera watched my movements, her expression impassive. But she didn't turn away again.

"I fucked up," I said softly. "Made a mess of everything. Eli died because of me, and I don't know how to deal with it. I don't know how to *live* with it." I gave a halfhearted shrug. "Most days, I don't want to."

My words sounded bleak and tasted like crumbling

ashes on my tongue, and yet it was a relief to confess even that much.

Thera turned a microfraction closer and I braced myself, ready for the stream of platitudes about better places and forgiving myself, or a torrent of cutting accusations of recklessness.

Instead she regarded me silently. "I'm not sure anyone knows how to live with something like that," she said after a moment. "You're just here, and that has to be enough for now."

"Because everything happens for a reason?" I asked. "Do you believe that?" The desperation in my voice made me cringe.

Her gaze skittered from mine. "I . . ."

"Never mind," I said. "That was dumb, forget it."

Thera sighed, slumping in her chair. "You want to know what Eli was doing?" she asked.

I looked up, hopeful.

"He was tutoring me," she said. "Because of my . . . other obligations, he had to come to my house. He thought your parents would probably not be too happy about that, so he—"

"He lied." That made infinitely more sense than any other scenario I'd come up with.

I leaned back and bumped my head against the cinderblock wall a couple of times. I was so stupid.

"He was my friend," Thera added.

"I'm sorry. For what I said. For this." I tipped my head toward Drizen's inner office. "I guess . . . I wanted there to be more. I wanted there to be some big secret. Something new to learn about him." I stared down at my left arm, trying to flex my fingers. "Because then it would be like he wasn't really gone, not yet."

"I think that's understandable," she said. "Kind of," she added with a hint of her original sharpness.

I felt the faint curve of a smile pulling at my mouth. She wasn't quite ready to let me off the hook. And that was fine; I deserved to be there.

Mrs. Clark rose from her desk and went to knock on Principal Drizen's door. He answered and she stuck her head in to speak with him, her hand gesturing toward Thera and me.

Time was almost up.

"Did you really mean what you said?" I asked Thera. "About your mom lying about what she does?"

Her mouth fell open slightly. "I don't . . ." She frowned. "Why?"

"I want to know if he's okay," I said, my voice gravelly and thick.

Understanding dawned, and her expression softened. "I don't know. I mean, there's something. She knows things she shouldn't. But if you're asking for proof, I can't help you there. I'm sorry."

The honesty hurt, but in some ways that was better than yet another attempt at comfort.

I nodded. "Thanks."

"Jacob?" Principal Drizen asked from his doorway, but his attention was focused on Thera. He shook his head at her with a sigh.

I stood up. "You going to be all right?" I asked her under my breath, as Drizen moved back to make room for me.

"Sure," she said. "Haven't you heard? This place is like my second home."

"I'll fix it," I said, taking a step toward Drizen's door.

She straightened up. "I don't need you to."

"Maybe it's not for you," I said quietly.

CHAPTER NINE

THE REST OF THE day dragged by, like I was slogging through knee-deep mud. Eli had been tutoring Thera. That was it. No secret, no hidden facet of his personality. And just like that, he was gone again. Relegated to memory.

It reminded me of acolyting. Once the wick on the taper was lit, you had to find a balance. Feed the flame too much wick and you'd risk it growing out of control. But if you kept the flame small, you were taking the chance that your movement might extinguish it.

Half the time as an acolyte, I'd moved too abruptly and the flame had flickered out before I made it to the other side of the altar.

In the principal's office, Drizen had greeted me with a handshake and a smile brimming with understanding, which made me want to scream.

But I could use it.

"I'm sorry for bothering you with this. It was a misunderstanding." I channeled my best Eli as I lowered myself into the chair in front of Drizen's desk. The hot seat normally, but today, Drizen was in compassionate-educator mode.

"I'm sure emotions were running high. I understand that your brother was a great help to her with her class work." Drizen paused. "Thera's not a bad kid."

But his tone indicated that he thought otherwise.

"She just forgets that not everything has to be a fight," he said, his mouth pinched with weariness and disapproval.

I wondered how often Thera had been in his office over the last year. And how hard she'd had to fight to get someone to listen to her. I wouldn't have listened before today.

"It wasn't her fault," I began. "I was—"

Principal Drizen waved his hand, dismissing my attempt at speech. "It doesn't matter. Thera put in a request to spend her exempt period in the library for additional hours as an aide, and I'm going to approve that. So it won't be a problem again."

Then, having received a final sympathetic pat on my shoulder and a pass to my next class, I was released back into the wild, with no idea what had happened.

Except that I felt like I'd lost something else. I just wasn't sure what it was. The only bright spot in my whole day had come from the two-second conversation that Thera and I had where we weren't yelling. When I'd blurted all that about not wanting to live with what I'd caused, she hadn't put on a fake smile in response or gotten that panicked, oh-shit expression. She'd thought about it and actually answered me.

I wished there could have been more of that.

Now, after an afternoon that had stretched into eternity, I limped out the front doors. My mom's minivan was nowhere in sight.

I frowned. That was weird. I couldn't drive while I was on pain pills, so she'd insisted on driving me everywhere, including to and from school. She didn't trust anyone else behind the wheel, particularly friends who might be distracted and get into another accident.

I dug in my pocket for my cell to see if I'd missed a call or text from her.

"Jace. Jacob!"

I searched faces and cars until I saw the open passenger-side window on the black Escalade hybrid, and the familiar figure behind the wheel summoning me with a sharp wave of his hand.

Dad.

My heart sank.

I lugged myself toward the Escalade. "What are you doing here?" I asked through the open window. Dad was in casual mode today; he wore a dark blue button-down shirt, with a tie instead of a formal clerical collar pressing tight against his neck.

"Your mother thought it would be good for you to start working at the church again, get back to another part of your routine," he said, staring straight ahead through the windshield. There was nothing to see but the dead brown grass and muddy patches of the baseball field in the distance.

It took me a second to run those words through the Parent Filter. Translation: My mom was pushing my dad and me together, hoping that would somehow make everything magically better.

Reluctantly I opened the door, releasing a wave of new leather smell from the pristine interior. Unlike my mom's van, which was frequently decorated with crushed Goldfish crackers, empty Gatorade bottles, and leftover streamers and poster paint from whatever project Eli had been working on, my dad's SUV was in factory condition.

The church paid the lease on it, so there was no eating or drinking in it and there was definitely no borrowing it. Even my mom didn't like to drive it, for fear that a gallon of milk would split open in the cargo area or that Sarah would barf in the backseat.

I hauled myself into the seat, shrugged out of my back-pack, and dropped it on the floor. It took me extra time to get my leg arranged around my bag, the door closed, and my seat belt on, and the entire time, I could feel the distance growing, like the driver's seat was moving far-ther and farther away from me. In the old days, before the accident, Dad would have asked me about my practice schedule, what the coaches were saying, if they were rec-ommending changes to my workout.

But now, without baseball, my dad and I didn't have much to talk about. Except all the things we *couldn't* talk about. And my healing injuries and impaired movements were vivid reminders of how everything had changed.

"Carol and Delores have been taking on the extra work, which is too much for them, especially during Lent," he said as he pulled away from the curb. "We need you to come back."

"I thought you would have hired someone else to take my place," I said. Or Eli's, at least. No matter what I did, the internship had been designed for two.

"You made a commitment to the council and to the Riverwoods community," my dad said.

Which meant if I didn't come back, it would be one more thing my dad would have to explain away.

I leaned my head against the headrest and closed my eyes.

My dad took a corner too quickly, and the force of it knocked my arm into the center console.

My eyes snapped open, watering, and I sucked in a sharp breath, my right hand moving reflexively to cover my elbow. The stitches were gone, and I was technically "healed" (after a second surgery to correct the first failed one). But tell that to the bones, ligaments, and muscles involved; they didn't seem to be getting the "all better" message.

Dad frowned, looking over at me for the first time. "Are you managing your pain medications appropriately?"

Because I'd screwed up in so many other ways.

Fury flashed through me but vanished before I could catch hold of it. "Yes," I said wearily.

"Are you sure?" my dad persisted.

This had to be coming from somewhere—probably from some well-meaning church member. "Dad—"

"You've lied to us before," my dad said, and the calmness in his voice was worse than if he'd yelled.

Line drive over the fence. No stopping that one.

I slumped in my seat. "If you think you can't trust me, then why are you asking?" I asked

"Because I'm trying, Jacob," he said, his knuckles blanching with his grip on the wheel. "I'm only asking that you do the same. You need to get back on track, Son."

How am I supposed to do that? I wanted to shout. When

he would never forgive me for not being Eli? When what little we had in common was gone? When I couldn't undo what I'd done? When I wasn't even sure if there was a point to any of this?

I turned away from him to stare out the side window.

"I have a counseling appointment," he said finally, as we pulled into the parking lot behind the new auditorium building. "Delores and Carol are expecting you in the office."

Then he parked the Escalade, stepped out, and smoothed his tie into place before walking away without looking back, leaving me to limp in on my own.

The good news was that the main offices for Riverwoods were now in the auditorium building. The building was much closer to the parking lot, and the auditorium was far less churchy than the main sanctuary, where we'd been on Sunday. No stained glass windows, polished pews, or candles. It was all modern: theater seating for a thousand, a stage, a giant metal sculpture representing the Dove of Peace—the Riverwoods logo—hanging on the center wall. Far less likely to trigger a panicked, existential freak-out in me. I hoped.

Outside the auditorium was a maze of hallways and offices and classrooms that might have been found in any school or corporate building. Except for the permanent bulletin board display of a cartoon Jesus with his hands outstretched in welcome to a diverse group of children, and the palm crosses from last year's Palm Sunday—now brown and dried—tacked to several wooden office doors, beneath the staff nameplates.

And yet, my shoulders tightened with dread as soon as I crossed the threshold and walked into what had been designated as the "greeting area." It still smelled like new carpeting and fresh paint, even after eight years.

This building had been Eli's home away from home. He'd helped my dad pick where his office would be, both of them well aware of the hope and expectation that it would one day be Eli's.

But the last time Eli had been here, it had been just his body, lifeless in a coffin on the auditorium stage.

I shut my eyes and shook my head, trying to clear the imagined image.

When I opened my eyes, a set of heavy wooden doors directly ahead of me caught my eye. On the other side of those doors, the quiet auditorium waited, and it felt like an ominous threatening presence.

The doors taunted me, daring me to face my sins and try to come out without further fracturing. But I was barely holding it together as it was.

With a deep breath, I turned away from the hypnotic pull of the doors and headed down the hallway that led to the central office. My dad's door was closed, the low murmur of voices escaping through the crack at the bottom as I passed.

I paused at the threshold of the central office area, which was humming with activity. The giant photocopying/collating/folding machine on the back wall was spitting out folded bulletins in a stack on the far right side. Carol, the office manager, was on the phone, arguing with someone, while Delores, my dad's personal admin, tapped at her keyboard, her long shiny red nails clicking loudly. Shelly, the administrative assistant for the directors of music, outreach, and children's programming, wasn't at her desk, but her aquarium screen saver burbled cheerfully, flashing tropical fish as they swam by.

Pastor Verner and Pastor Matthews, both of whom reported to my dad, had offices and assistants on the other side of the building, which was probably a statement of some kind. My dad keeping them at a distance, literally and figuratively? After all, the only way to get promoted at Riverwoods, as far as I knew, was to leave and take a new call, or to try to force the head pastor out in a polite, socially acceptable coup. Dad wasn't taking any chances.

"You're back!" Delores exclaimed, pushing back from her desk as I walked in.

Carol waved and smiled at me before scowling at the paperwork in front of her. "No, we changed this order months ago," she said into the phone, rolling her eyes. "Four hundred lilies. I have the confirmation number right here."

"Let me help you with that, honey." Delores came around the edge of her desk, reaching to take my backpack. Delores had been working for my dad for as long as I could remember. She was kind of a third grandma, with big hair, wicked nails, and more jewelry than one of those gold exchange stores.

"No, I got it," I said with a lame smile, holding my bag closer like a shield.

It would keep her from trying to hug me. I didn't want to hurt her feelings, but I just couldn't let her do that. The familiar smell of her rose perfume would bring back a thousand memories, most of them with Eli at my side. And if I knew her, she'd start crying, and then I'd be caught in that awful position of making her uncomfortable for crying when I wasn't crying myself. I couldn't cry anymore; it hurt too much. And terrible as it sounded, I didn't have enough emotional energy left to soothe another grieving person.

As if sensing my reluctance, Delores retreated, fidgeting with the series of gold bracelets on her wrist. "I'm so glad you're back, honey." Her heavily mascaraed eyelashes left dark, damp spots beneath her eyes when she blinked back her tears. "And that you're doing okay." She pressed her hands to her chest. "We were so worried about you."

Eli's absence loomed, overshadowing every word.

I nodded and forced myself to smile again. "Thanks. I'm doing all right now."

Her mouth turned down, which told me she recognized the words for the lie they were. But she didn't call me on it.

"Well, good." She squeezed my shoulder. I tried not to flinch but wasn't entirely successful.

Her gaze jumped away from mine, hurt radiating from her.

Crap.

"Shelly got the bulletins started for us," she said. "But if you want to take over with the inserts, that would be real helpful."

She gestured awkwardly toward the desk in the far corner of the office, the same one Eli and I had shared, as if I didn't remember. But there was only one chair at the desk now, the good one.

I searched for the other chair and found it in the opposite corner, near the giant photocopier. Reams of paper had been stacked on the seat along with foam boards depicting what appeared to be a series of buildings—probably my dad's latest church expansion dreams—as if these items would disguise it.

I appreciated the effort. But seeing the bad chair,

alone and in the corner, felt like a punch to the chest. That stupid chair. Eli and I had had an unspoken game to see who would get stuck with it. Whoever got to the office first claimed the good one. But if you left it, you didn't get it back.

It was stupid but just something we did. Hell, we'd never even talked about it. And now it was over. One of a million little important things that would sound so insignificant if I tried to explain. Was I mourning my brother's life cut so short? Grieving that he'd never be my best man, or that we'd never have a chance to try to trick any kids or nieces or nephews we might have had by switching places?

Nope, I was sad about a dumb chair.

I made my way over to the intern desk and sat in the good chair. Delores brought over a batch of bulletins and inserts. "Here. This should get you started." She reached out to pat my shoulder and stopped herself.

Before she could walk away, I reached back with my good hand and caught hers, giving it a quick, clumsy squeeze. "Thanks."

"Of course, honey," she said, her voice quavering with emotion. Then she bustled to her desk, where she blew her nose loudly. "Allergies," she announced to the entire office.

I smiled and turned my attention to the inserts and pale purple bulletins in front of me. The only artwork was text in a simple, scrolling font: "Create in me a clean heart, O God."

The words sent a strange pang through me. I couldn't tell if it was from recognizing my own need in them or from recognizing that the need was likely to remain unanswered.

I was almost done assembling the stack when the phone rang. Delores answered. "Riverwoods Bible . . . Carrie? Is everything okay?"

Mom. My head popped up. I could hear someone shrieking or crying through the receiver from across the room.

"Is that my mom?" I asked, standing, dread suffusing my whole body. Once something awful has happened, you assume the worst every time after that.

At her desk, Carol looked up from her computer, her forehead crinkling into worried lines.

"No, he's in a counseling appointment right now," Delores said, gripping the receiver tighter, her rings making a scraping noise against the plastic. "But, Carrie, I can . . . Let me get him if it's an emergency."

"What's going on?" I asked.

Carol stood and started for my dad's door. But Delores held her hand up to stop her.

Delores's gaze flicked to me. "Yes, he's here. . . . I don't know. I didn't hear it ring. He's . . . Just a second." She held the receiver out to me.

I hurried to Delores's desk. "Mom, what's wrong?"

"Why didn't you answer your phone?" she asked.

I reached for my phone in my pocket and checked the screen. Five missed calls from home. "I forgot to take it off silent," I said. I'd been so distracted by my dad's unexpected arrival, I'd completely blown past my regular post-school ritual.

"What's going on?" I asked, shoving my phone back in my pocket. "Is that Sarah?" It sounded more like a wounded animal than a person. I'd never heard her cry like that, not even after Eli died.

"Yes," my mom said, sounding more tired and frustrated than upset. "When she asked why we weren't going to get you today after school, I told her we didn't have to. And then she lost it."

There was the sound of fabric rustling and my mom's muffled voice as she turned away from the phone. "Sarah, please, I'm talking to Jace right now." The desperation in her tone came through loud and clear. "He's okay, I told you."

"I told her you were at the church," she said to me. "She doesn't believe me."

Because the last time her brothers hadn't been where they were supposed to be, Sarah had learned that one of us was dead.

"She's crying so hard, she's going to make herself

sick. But I can't get her out from under her bed."

"Do you think she might need some help?" I asked carefully, aware that other people were listening. But what I meant was: She needs a therapist. I'd thought it before, but never dared to say anything. For that matter, we should probably all have one.

"Jace," my mom said sharply. "Everyone grieves differently."

There was a world of reprimand in those words. My dad was a counselor; he didn't get counseled. So I guess neither did the rest of us. When your primary spiritual advisor was also a member of your family—the same member who was currently working very hard to keep up appearances—then it was kind of a major conflict of interest and impossible to make any headway.

I'm so tired of this. I rubbed my forehead with my free hand. Tired of being careful, tired of not being able to say what really needed to be said.

"You want me to try to talk to her?" I asked, not sure what else to say.

My mom didn't answer me, but I heard her talking to Sarah. "Honey, Jace is on the phone. I told you we'd find him. He wants to talk to you."

"Sares, it's me," I said, raising my voice a little. "What's wrong?"

No response but more wailing.

I grimaced. I wasn't sure she could hear me over the noise she was making.

"Sarah," I shouted into the phone, like I was bellowing at her for messing with the TV settings. She liked to turn people green and red with the tint/brightness controls on the remote.

The sobbing on the other end of the line paused for a moment, followed by a hiccup.

"Jace?" a small, wobbly voice asked.

I exhaled. "Yeah, it's me. What's wrong?"

"You're not dead. Where are you?" she asked, sounding pitiful.

"No, I'm not dead. I'm at the church, like Mom said. Are you okay?"

"With Dad?" she persisted.

"Yeah."

"Are you sure?" she asked, her voice trembling.

"Yes, Sarah, I'm sure," I said, trying not to let my frustration leak through. I wasn't mad at her; it was the entire situation that was so messed up. "I'm standing right here in the office next to Delores and Carol." Who had both returned to their work, pretending not to hear every word of the conversation. "Do you need me to come home?"

"No," she said quickly. "I'm okay. Don't come home."

"Sarah—"

But a loud clunk came through the receiver, and then more rustling noises.

"Sarah," my mom said, her voice muffled. "You talked to Jace. Don't you want to come out now?"

My mom sighed, a long sad sound, and then spoke to me, her words clearer and more distinct. "She's stopped crying now, at least. But she's refusing to come out from under the bed."

A fresh wave of guilt pummeled me.

"Do you want me to come home?" I asked.

"I can't leave her here to—"

"I can find a ride."

In the silence, I could sense my mom weighing the pros and cons. Carol and Delores would never say anything about this, but my dad would be upset that our personal life had once again spilled all over church grounds. If I left without finishing the work I'd been assigned, that would only make it worse.

"No," my mom said finally. "Stay there, finish working. She's calmer now."

"Are you sure?" I asked.

"Yes," she said, sounding more certain. "Dad will bring you home when he comes back for dinner before his meetings tonight. It's only a couple more hours. She'll be fine for that long. I'll have to eat those gummy bears I found all by myself." That last was pitched away from me and toward Sarah.

"Thanks, honey," she said to me, distracted. "We'll see you when you get home." The phone clicked in my ear.

My shoulders sagged, aching with the release of tension I hadn't felt until that second.

I handed the phone to Delores, and she busied herself with untangling the cord.

I clenched my fists against the rage and despair pushing up from my stomach, as if they were something I could actually fight. Why did we always have to pretend everything was okay? Why couldn't we just admit that we were falling apart? If we couldn't do that, I wasn't sure how we were going to get better.

"Jace?" Delores asked from behind me, her voice full of worry.

"Yeah, I'm fine," I said grimly. What else was there to say?

CHAPTER TEN

"HEY!"

A french fry bounced off my cheek and landed in the congealing grease on my pizza slice.

I looked up from my tray, startled.

"What's up, bro?" Zach asked, as he wiped his hands on a napkin. "I called your name, like, three times."

"Just tired," I said. "Long day."

A burst of laughter came from the other end of our cafeteria table, where Caleb, Derek, Scott, and Matt were all talking about something that seemed to involve fireworks and a poorly placed sofa cushion.

"There's tired, and then there's the walking dead," Zach said around a mouthful of burger. "You are the latter today, my friend. What's up?"

Audrey gave a nervous bark of laughter, pushing her hair back from her face. "Zach."

I shook my head, negating her concern over Zach's choice of words.

My anger from yesterday afternoon had faded, leaving a heavy gray haze over everything. My dad had driven me home in a mutual tense silence. Then the three of us had taken turns trying to talk Sarah into coming out from under the bed. I'd listened to my parents alternate threats with cajoling, getting nowhere.

When it was my turn, I sat next to the bed so she knew I was there. I had no idea what was going on in her little head. I could hear the sound of her crayons scribbling across paper, though. Maybe she, like me, couldn't talk about it yet. Or ever.

But no matter what, sometimes it was nice to know that another person was nearby. That you weren't alone.

I stayed until my leg began to ache from sitting in one position, and then when I started to get up, Sarah's hand appeared from under the bed ruffle, patted the back of my hand twice—as if she were the one comforting me—and then vanished again.

It wasn't much, but it was something.

Then, this morning, she'd been back to her ghost routine, drifting through the house in her pajamas, with

Patsie and blanket in hand. But neither of my parents had complained, because she'd crawled out from under the bed, eaten a bowl of cereal, and gotten dressed for school, all without argument and while still avoiding me. Sarah needed help. But I couldn't get my mom and dad to see it.

If Eli had been here, I would have been able to tell him and he would have figured out how to bring it up, what to say to get them to understand. But then again, if Eli had been here, none of this would have been an issue.

"What do you think happens after you die?" I asked Audrey and Zach.

Their shocked silence was louder, for a moment, than all the noise of the cafeteria around us.

"Sarah freaked out yesterday," I continued. "About Eli, I think. I'm trying to figure out what to tell her, how to help her. But everyone keeps talking about heaven or being in a 'better place.' And I just . . . I'm not sure."

Zach and Audrey exchanged uncertain glances; then Zach forced an uncomfortable laugh. "Isn't this kind of your dad's territory?"

I shrugged.

Audrey set her fork down on her tray and reached out to pat my shoulder hesitantly. "I'm sure Eli is okay, wherever he is, Jace. And Sarah will understand that eventually."

"Yeah." Zach nodded vigorously, his hair flopping in his eyes.

"The most important thing is that you remember him and keep him a part of your life that way," Audrey added. "That's how you help Sarah."

It sounded so familiar, the same thing everyone said at every funeral ever. To the point of being meaningless.

"You can't let yourself get caught up in this stuff. You gotta focus on being here, being alive," Zach said. "That's what Eli would want you to do."

Was it? My brother was dead, and it was possible he wasn't in a better place, that he was just gone. No one seemed willing to discuss that possibility.

Except, maybe, Thera Catoulus.

I'd missed her presence in Pussy PE—in Exempt today.

I kept looking to her seat, registering her absence, in the same way you poke your tongue at the soft, sore spot left behind when a tooth falls out.

I wasn't sure what I wanted from her, or why I felt a pull toward her. What was it about her?

It was clear she despised me and what I'd done to Eli. I should be staying as far from her as possible. What kind of idiot would seek that hatred out?

"Maybe you're right," I said finally. But it didn't *feel* right. That's what was tripping me up. Though these days, very little felt right.

After another awkward gap in conversation, Audrey sat up straighter in her chair, as if she were taking charge of a poorly run meeting.

"So. We should talk about Spring Formal," she announced.

Zach groaned, which earned him a shoulder smack.

"It's only seven weeks away," she said. "We need to start making plans."

Just like that, the conversation about Eli was over. I couldn't blame Audrey and Zach; before the accident, I wouldn't have wanted to talk about this either. Actually, I would have actively avoided it.

"You're the one who needs to make plans. Dress shopping, hair appointments . . ." Zach waved his hand dismissively. "I've got the rest of it figured out."

"Really?" Audrey asked suspiciously.

"Sure." He shrugged. "I'll borrow the family roadster—more space for everyone—and then we'll hit up that crappy drive-in place Jace loves."

I listened to them, feeling oddly removed from the moment, like I was watching it on a movie screen.

Audrey narrowed her eyes at Zach. "You'd better be kidding."

Zach held his hands up in defense. "Yes, I'm kidding," he said with some exasperation. "But you know Coach is going to have us in practice until the last second, right?"

He looked to me for support before realizing his mistake.

He and Audrey froze, looking stricken. "Sorry, bro," Zach managed after a moment.

"It's okay," I said. "I wasn't much for dancing before anyway. Now I might actually hurt someone else or myself." I clunked my cast against the floor carefully for emphasis.

They laughed, as I'd intended them to, and the tension disappeared. But instead of sharing in their relief, I felt more alone. The gap between us was only growing wider. It was a truth I'd been trying to ignore for the last couple of days, digging in like a splinter: I didn't belong here anymore.

The person I'd been before the accident was gone, and there was no getting him back.

CHAPTER ELEVEN

WEDNESDAY EVENING LENTEN SERVICES weren't well attended, which was why we were at the original church building rather than the auditorium. The organ played intro music, the sound muted so as not to drown out the various preservice conversations. My mom, Sarah, and I were earlier than we'd been on Sunday; the narthex was filled with people chatting with one another before they took a seat.

So far, I wasn't feeling the rush of sickening panic—like I was falling face-first into a gaping chasm and couldn't catch myself—that I'd felt on Sunday. That was something, at least.

I watched the smiling faces around me, some of them more lined with worry or stress than others, as we moved closer to the sanctuary.

They belonged here. They felt safe and comforted. Crap might be raining down on other aspects of their lives, but being here made them feel better and offered reassurance.

My eyes burning, I turned away from the sanctuary, focusing my attention on something—anything—else.

The architectural drawings that I'd seen in the church office yesterday were now propped on discreetly placed easels. I pretended to study the drawings on the easel near the outside doors, though from where I stood I could make out little more than big squares that obviously indicated new buildings, and a couple of words here and there. "Community Center." "Bookstore." "Parking Structure." "Coffeehouse."

"Hey." A hand touched mine.

I turned to find Leah at my side. She was dressed in a black cardigan and skirt, similar to what my mom was wearing. I wondered if that was intentional.

She was also standing too close to me.

"Leah. Hey." I took an awkward step back to put space between us, my cast catching on a grout line in the tile and causing me to stumble even farther from her.

She frowned. "Are you—"

"Yes, fine," I said, more sharply than I should have.

Her gaze skated over my face, searching for truth and not finding it.

"How are you?" I asked, redirecting the conversation before she could push. And knowing Leah, whether the old one or the new one who was trying to be my friend, she would push.

Her eyes watered, and I regretted the question. "I'm all right. Some moments are better than others." She smiled bravely. "I mean, *you* know."

I did, but it wasn't something I wanted to discuss with her. She wouldn't understand my doubts and fears. When Leah had come over the other day and asked me to talk about Eli sometimes, I'd thought she meant things like his annoying tendency to eat food "in order"—chips from the most seasoning to the least, Skittles by color, and in clockwise sequence on his plate—or how he analyzed movies to death in search of a theme.

But Leah had obviously interpreted our conversation differently.

"I wondered if it would be okay if I sat with you guys tonight?" she asked, biting her lip.

Automatically, I looked over my shoulder at my mom. She and Sarah were about to go into the sanctuary.

My mom turned then, looking back for me to join them. But when she noticed Leah next to me, she caught my eye and nodded, unspoken permission to continue my conversation. She bent down and whispered something to Sarah, and the two of them crossed into the sanctuary.

"Uh, sure," I said to Leah. Under my shirt, my back grew sticky with sweat. At this point, I was still trying to convince myself that I could walk in and take a seat. With Leah there, sad-faced and wanting to share, I wasn't sure I could be in the building.

"I know, it's not the same." Leah took a deep breath and let it out slowly. "But I feel so close to him here. I know he's watching over us." She looked up at the ceiling with a smile. "Don't you feel him here?"

It was hard to feel anything at the moment except the constriction in my chest.

"Uh-huh," I managed.

"I think he'll like seeing us all together," Leah continued. "Knowing that we have each other to get us through."

I looked away from Leah, staring blindly at the building drawings again.

This time, through the sidelight window behind the easel, I caught the faintest hint of a blue glow. The blue neon palm had not been lit when we'd come in from the parking lot, but, with Psychic Mary's usual timing, it was now.

Thera.

The thought of her, angry and snarling at me at first, and then saying all the things that no one else would, made the tightness in my lungs ease slightly.

I moved away from Leah and toward the exit before I had time to think about it.

"Jace?" she asked with a confused frown.

"Yeah, just . . . I need some air. Go ahead. I'll meet you in there." I fumbled for a smile, trying to make it believable.

"All right," she said uncertainly.

I took the opportunity and the seminatural break in the excruciating conversation to make a stilted run for the doors.

I didn't care if it was rude. I needed out.

Pushing the door open, I stepped outside. It was sleeting now, and the little bits of ice bounced off my face and down the collar of my shirt, melting instantly.

With a solid thunk, the church door closed behind me.

I inhaled deeply. The air was so sharp with cold that it hurt, but it wasn't enough to dispel the tension thrumming through me.

I took one step down, and then another, half expecting to hear the doors open behind me, someone calling my name. The equivalent of a lightning bolt or a sign from above to stop me. But the only sound was the clinking hiss of the sleet hitting the ground, and my shoe and casted foot crunching in it, moving faster than they had in weeks.

The road was dark and empty, traffic a distant hum at the intersection down the block, so it only took me a few seconds to cross the street and climb the sagging porch stairs.

My hand shaking, I pressed the doorbell. But there was no sound inside, no echo of the bell.

I knocked on the splintery wooden door, white paint flecks raining down on the worn welcome mat below.

"Come on, come on," I whispered.

The curtain on the window next to the door fluttered, revealing a flash of dark hair and pale skin.

But the door didn't open.

I knocked again, a little harder this time, and the sound of a dead bolt retracting finally greeted me.

I lowered my hand, and the hinges squealed in protest as Thera pulled the door back. "I tried the doorbell," I said.

"It doesn't work," Thera said. "What are you doing here?" She shivered and folded her arms across her chest. She wasn't dressed for outside, wearing only a tank top and boxer shorts, and I could see the goose bumps rising on her skin. "Don't you have somewhere else to be?" she asked, tipping her head toward the church behind me. Even out here I could hear the organ music. The opening hymn, most likely.

An excellent question. What exactly had I come for? Now that I was here, I wasn't sure anymore. "No, I wanted to . . ." I stuffed my hands into the pockets of my khakis. "I guess I wanted to talk."

"About what?" she asked, taking a step back, as if

preparing to shut the door on me. "If this is about Eli again, I don't have—"

"I died," I said, the words startling me in their starkness. I'd never said them out loud, not to anyone.

Her mouth opened in surprise, and she went still.

"That night in the car. It wasn't just Eli. I died too. For a few minutes. They brought me back," I said, my voice catching.

The wind, sweeping under the porch roof, blasted pellets of sleet at us. Thera wrapped her arms tighter around herself but didn't retreat.

"I didn't see anything, though," I said, studying the hinges of the door. Saying these words aloud felt like speaking in a foreign language for the first time; I wasn't sure what I was doing, nothing felt familiar or right. "When I was gone, there was just nothing. Blackness."

My throat swelled with all the emotion I'd been fighting to keep down. "And then, when I woke up and they told me Eli was dead, I realized . . ." I worked my jaw back and forth, trying to get a grip on my runaway feelings. "I realized I'd done that to him. I got my brother killed, and worse than that, if what I saw is right, I made him not exist. Not here, not in heaven, not anywhere."

The last word exploded out of me in a gasp, and tears—ones I wasn't allowed to shed because this was all my fault—overflowed, hot on my face.

Thera was quiet for a moment. Then she squared her shoulders, seeming to come to a decision.

"Come on." She reached out and caught my wrist, tugging me across the threshold.

CHAPTER TWELVE

THE ENTRYWAY OF THERA'S house smelled of cookies and something flowery.

I rubbed my sleeve over my eyes to get rid of the tears, but my throat felt raw and full in a way that suggested they might start again anytime.

Thera shut and locked the door behind me, holding a finger up to her lips. "She's with a phone client," she said, tipping her head toward the closed pocket doors to my right. I could hear the faint murmur of a female voice beyond them.

"This way." Thera moved around me and then started up the stairs, her bare feet light on the worn wooden treads.

Out of habit, I wiped my feet on the mat, then followed her. Lots of framed photos decorated the wall on the way up, covering but not hiding the faded and peeling wallpaper. Everything here seemed old, but not messy or dirty, unlike the outside of their house. Nothing screamed "paranormal" here either. No Ouija boards or crystal balls that I could see, no strange symbols painted on the walls.

At the top of the stairs, Thera walked into the only lit room.

I stopped in the doorway. The room was small, with angles in the ceiling that made it feel even smaller, and the bed, covered in a quilt and a tidy assortment of textbooks and notebooks, dominated the space. A brightly colored rag rug, flattened and dulled by time and use, lay right by the bed. Pages torn out of magazines and books—at a quick glance, they all appeared to be photos or sketches of bridges—were taped to the slanted ceiling, right above where it met the walls. But the windows were old and big, so the overall effect wasn't so much claustrophobic as cozy, a hideaway from the world. It wasn't anything like what I'd expected from her, not that I had any specific idea of what to expect.

"Come in," Thera said. "Sit there." She pointed to a heavy wooden rocker in the corner. "I'll get you a towel."

She disappeared into the hallway, her feet padding softly on the floor, before I could respond.

I dropped into the rocker, scrubbing my hands over my face. My eyes felt hot and swollen.

Thera returned in a few seconds. "Here." She passed me a towel, green and soft-looking, with frayed edges.

"I'm sorry," I said, as she retreated to sit on the edge of her bed. "I'm not sure what I'm doing here. I just couldn't be over there anymore, and I didn't know where else to go." Said aloud, it sounded ridiculous. Like Thera would somehow have answers to questions I barely had the words to express.

A trickle of icy water from the now melting sleet ran down the back of my neck and under my collar. I shivered.

Thera stood with a sigh and took the towel from my hands, then moved between my knees.

"I don't know what happened to Eli," she said quietly. With quick but gentle movements, she rubbed the towel over my head and down my neck. "I don't know if anyone can really know for sure."

After the accident, I'd fought for months to regain my independence in everything, from walking unassisted to showering without one of those old-person bath seats. Asking for help always felt like being a burden on someone else, and when it came to my family, I'd already caused so much pain and trouble, I didn't want to add to it any more than necessary. I didn't want to make them care for me when they blamed me.

But it felt so good to be touched, I had to curl my hands into fists to keep from reaching out to pull Thera closer. I didn't realize how long it had been since I'd felt that connection with another living person.

"But on the really bad days, when I'm struggling and wondering if there's a point to any of this," she said, "those are the days that I remind myself about the sun."

"What, that it will come out tomorrow?" I asked.

She retreated with a snort, taking the towel with her. "No," she said, settling on the foot of her bed. With the room as small as it was, I could still reach out and touch her. "It takes, like, eight minutes for light to reach Earth from the sun. But it's instantaneous to us here."

Hello, science. She was a science nerd. I never would have guessed that.

"We don't even think about it," she said, tucking her hair behind her ears as she warmed to the topic. "It's easy to forget that we're one little planet in the distant corner of a huge galaxy and that there probably are other life-forms out there, but not like us. Not exactly like us, anyway. They have problems too, whoever they are. We, in our tiny corner of the universe, don't understand everything, not even half of what we *know* about, let alone what we're still discovering. So—"

"So what's one person dying in all of that?" I asked bitterly. "That's what you're saying."

"Not at all," she said. "I'm saying that the world or existence or whatever is bigger than we allow ourselves to think. Which means that no matter what, we're only seeing part of the picture. Individual pixels. What looks like the end or like meaningless and painful chaos might just mean we're too close to the screen to understand."

Pain tightened her voice, and her gaze dropped to focus on the towel in her lap as she folded it, matching the raggedy edges precisely.

Immediately, my mind flashed to her in the hall yesterday, Caleb stalking alongside her, trying to touch her hair. How she'd slapped his hand away and picked up her pace.

What had the rest of her day been like? What was the rest of her life like?

I cleared my throat. "So you like bridges?"

Her hands paused, and she looked up. "Yeah."

"Which one is your favorite?" I gestured to her ceiling.

"Uh, which picture or which bridge?" she asked.

"Both."

She stood and moved around to the side of the bed to point at a black-and-white photo in the center of the ceiling. "The Juscelino Kubitschek Bridge in Brazil," she said. "My favorite picture."

I got up to get a better look at it. The photo showed a side view of a bridge at night, the angled arches glowing like silver.

Thera had stayed where she was, her toes curling on the rag rug. Her arm brushed my sleeve, and I could smell the soft, minty scent of her hair. If she turned toward me, we'd be almost eye to eye. Mouth to mouth.

I took a deep breath. "And your favorite in general?" I asked.

"My favorite in general is the da Vinci bridge. It's a footbridge in Norway." She moved around me carefully to point at a color print hanging above the rocker where I'd sat, probably exactly where she could see it from bed. "The builders followed da Vinci's original plans on a reduced scale; it opened in 2001. The plans are centuries old, but it looks like something that could have been designed today." Her voice held awe and admiration.

"So this is your thing," I said. Like baseball had been for me.

"I want to build them," she said, raising her chin in challenge.

"Architect?" I asked.

"Engineer," she muttered. "If I can ever get out of here."

Thera sat back down on the bed.

I started toward the chair, but she moved a pile of notes to make room for me. "Here," she said, nodding at the now cleared space.

Careful to keep distance between us, I sank down next to her.

"I miss him," I admitted, my voice gritty. "So much.

But I can't say that to most people because—"

"You can miss him, no matter what. You're allowed," she said fiercely.

I nodded, my stupid eyes overflowing again. "You want to tell everyone else that?" I managed, forcing a laugh as I wiped my face with the heel of my hand.

She shrugged. "If you need me to," she said with a small smile. And it wouldn't surprise me if she did it. She was a fighter.

Lowering my head, I closed my eyes and pressed my fingers against the lids. "I don't know what I'm doing."

Thera bumped me gently with her elbow. "There's no right way to miss someone. It's a hole on the inside. You can't fix that. You just live through it until one day the edges of the hole aren't so sharp." The ache of experience resonated through her words.

I opened my eyes to look at her. "Who?"

"My grandparents," she said. "They were . . . normal." She gave me a rueful smile. "Mostly, anyway. When they were alive, my life was better. They gave my mom total shit for what she is, what she does, and that wasn't so great." Thera shrugged. "But regular meals, money to buy a new lawn mower or fix the leaky faucet, a reliable roof over our heads . . ." She sighed. "I don't know."

I did. She was as trapped by her mother's choices as

I was by my dad's, choices that had been made before we were born.

Against my better judgment, I reached out to touch the back of her hand, half expecting her to jolt away or slap at me, as she had Caleb.

But to my surprise, after a second of hesitation, she turned her palm up and caught my fingers in hers. Her gaze held mine, and that feeling of connection between us pulled tight.

Following it, I leaned in. The warmth of her breath and the minty scent of her hair surrounded me. I brushed my mouth over hers, and her lips were soft beneath mine, shaking a little as she kissed me back.

But she slid away almost immediately, releasing my hand.

It took me a second to process what had happened. "Sorry," I said, my face hot. "I shouldn't have . . . That was—"

"It's okay." But she wouldn't look at me.

I'd screwed up. Again.

An awkward silence descended. I could hear a radiator wheezing to life somewhere nearby.

"I should get back," I said. "Services are shorter on Wednesdays."

She nodded. "You don't want anyone to know that you're over here."

I winced, though her tone held no judgment. "Yeah. It's—"

"Complicated," she said, climbing off the bed. "I know."

Of course she did. Eli had already told her all about it.

Jealousy clawed at me.

I shook my head. Stupid. It was only tutoring. But I liked Thera. And she and Eli had obviously been close, a closeness I couldn't hope to replicate. Eli was Eli, and that wasn't me. Much to everyone's regret.

Thera led the way out of the room and down the stairs.

I followed, but at the door, I stopped. "Thank you." The words were completely inadequate in exchange for the first moment in months where I hadn't felt completely alone—before I'd messed it up—but they were all I had.

Thera folded her arms, moving her foot across the floor in the pattern of the faded flowered rug. "You're welcome."

"You know you could come back to Pussy—to Exempt, if you wanted to," I said.

She gave an easy shrug. "Nah, the library's okay. I have friends in there most of the time, and more aide hours is better for my college applications anyway. I just couldn't get them to approve it before."

I nodded. "Okay, so I guess . . . I'll see you." The idea of not knowing *when* I would see or talk to her again for sure created a hollow space inside me.

She pulled the door open for me and stepped back. "Yeah."

But as I walked out the door and onto the porch, she drew in a breath. "Jace . . ."

I turned to face her, and an emotion that I couldn't identify flickered across her face, furrowing her forehead, before vanishing.

Then she shook her head. "Good night," she said simply, and closed the door.

CHAPTER THIRTEEN

I SHOULDN'T HAVE KISSED HER. Stupid.

I thumped the back of my head against the exposed brick wall of the narthex.

After Thera had closed her door, I'd slipped back into the church. Judging by the prayers in progress, the service was about ten minutes from the end. The ushers had long since entered the sanctuary, and with any luck, no one would know how long I'd been gone, or where.

Listening to the beginning notes of the final hymn, I leaned against the wall and shifted my weight off my bad leg, which was throbbing from effort and the cold.

It had been worth it, though. Just saying the words aloud—*I died*—had lifted an enormous burden. And Thera hadn't taken offense at my questions or doubts. Hadn't seemed even vaguely threatened. If anything, doubting and questioning appeared to be a regular part of her thought process.

You hear about people being described as a breath of fresh air, but I'd never understood how much that actually meant in the context of suffocating slowly in a thick, stale, unbreathable atmosphere.

With Thera, I could breathe. I could ask. I could argue. It made me almost shaky with relief, the pressure relieved, if only temporarily.

And then I had to mess things up.

There was nothing like asking a girl if she was secretly involved with your brother one day and then trying to kiss her the next. God.

I'd have to find her tomorrow, try to apologize again. I didn't want to lose . . . whatever that was. However you defined it, those few moments with her had been the easiest, least complicated minutes of my life in months.

The ushers came out and opened the doors to the sanctuary, and I straightened up, pretending to have been there for a while. Like I'd left to use the bathroom and hadn't wanted to disrupt the last of the service by going back in.

"Jace! There you are," my mom said when she emerged from the crowd, relief written on her face. "You were sitting with Leah?"

"Uh . . ." Leah hadn't joined them? "I didn't . . ."

But my mom was giving me a warning look. "I told Sarah that's where you were," my mom said, with that "don't mess this up" tone in her voice.

My gaze dropped to my sister, who was holding my mom's hand and carefully avoiding making eye contact with me.

"Yep. I sat with Leah."

Hopefully my mom and Leah wouldn't compare stories about where I was and was not.

Huh. Maybe Eli and I were more alike than I realized.

"Come on, Sarah!" my mom called in the direction of the dining room. "We're having late night special, and I need *you* to pick out which cookie cutter we're going to use." It was a bribe, an obvious one. Then she turned to me. "Jacob, bowls."

Late night special was a tradition on Wednesday nights during Lent. Usually tomato soup and grilled cheeses, cut into shapes.

When Eli and I were younger, we'd fought over whose turn it was to choose the shape. But once Sarah turned four, we'd handed over that responsibility to her. She'd taken it on with glee, choosing the most ridiculous cookie cutters.

But I doubted that making everyone's sandwiches look like ghosts or candy canes was the enticement it had once been. Still, my mom was trying.

The familiar smell of toasting bread was comforting, as was the clank of the skillet against the burner. It could have been a scene from any night in my life over the last few years.

I crossed to the cabinet and pulled down four bowls. I was halfway to the dining room before I realized what I'd done: grabbed four automatically and without thought, as I used to grab five. It was the first time since Eli's death that I'd done that.

I froze, teetering on the sharp edge of relief and a double-portion of guilt. Relief that maybe Thera was right and that Eli's death wouldn't always hurt this much, that one day it wouldn't be the central focus of my life. Guilt because Eli was dead and it should hurt. I was alive; I didn't deserve relief.

"Jacob, honey?" Mom asked. She was watching me closely, the spatula in her hand. "What's wrong?"

"I'm fine, I just . . ." I held up the bowls. "I only took four."

Her expression softened.

"It's all right," she said gently. "Life goes on eventually. It's supposed to happen that way. He wants that for us, I'm sure."

I wasn't sure Eli wanted anything anymore.

The garage door went up, and we both automatically looked toward the mudroom.

"Dad's home early," my mom said with surprise. "Sarah, I need you to come now! Otherwise I'm going to make them all circles."

I took the bowls into the dining room, and was heading for the silverware drawer in the kitchen when my dad's footsteps sounded behind me, too loud and too close. I moved to get out of the way, thinking I'd crossed in front of him accidentally.

But then his hand caught tight around my collar, hauling me backward. My arms windmilled as I tried to keep my balance.

"Micah!" My mom sounded shocked.

"What is wrong with you?" he demanded through clenched teeth, his voice right next to my ear.

"I don't . . . What?" I asked, my heart catapulting into triple time. My dad had never laid a hand on any of us.

"Are you trying to make things worse?" He shook me a little and then let go.

I stumbled to the side, catching myself on the edge of the island to keep my footing, and then turned to gape at him. His face was flushed above his blue shirt and white clerical collar, and his dark hair was rumpled.

"What is going on?" my mom demanded, rushing around the island to stand next to me.

"Would you like to explain to me where you were during service tonight?" he asked in a too calm voice that was somehow more frightening than when he'd grabbed me a moment ago.

Crap.

Instinctively, I looked to my mother for help, but she was staring wide-eyed at my dad, like she'd never seen him before. "He was sitting with Leah, Micah. I don't think that's cause for *this*."

"Is that right? Because Leah told me she saw you go across the street," he said.

My mom sucked in a breath. "Across the street" was code for Psychic Mary's.

"You're lucky it was Leah," he said, jabbing a finger in my direction. "She stopped me after service and told me in confidence. If she'd told her father instead, do you have any idea how much trouble that would have caused?"

I grimaced. Mr. Hauer was definitely the most conservative of the church council members, and he was the president. My dad would never have heard the end of it.

But why was it always about everyone else? It wasn't that my dad didn't want me over there, though I was sure he didn't, or even that he believed all the stupid whispered rumors about "consorting with dark forces" or whatever.

It was about Mr. Hauer and the church. As always. It didn't matter if we were struggling or falling apart or pushed to desperate measures. Appearances were all that mattered.

My temper flickered to life and, for the first time in months, caught hold. "Yeah, because that's the worst part about all of this, what everyone at church will think."

"Jacob—" my mom tried.

"It's not a big deal," I argued. "Thera and I are in the same class at school."

"And you felt the need to go over there in the middle of service because . . . ?" my dad pressed.

"Thera's not the devil incarnate, no matter what Mr. Hauer might say," I said, avoiding the question. "She and her mom . . . they're just people."

"It doesn't matter," my dad said. "At a minimum, they're criminals and con artists, and by going there, you're undermining my authority. I'm trying to convince the council and the congregation to push against the city and commit millions of dollars for this expansion based on my vision and my leadership, and my kid is across the street, chatting up the enemy."

The enemy?

"After a loss, I think it's normal to look at the world a little differently," my mom offered tentatively, making eye contact with me for the first time and giving me an understanding nod. "And the desire to reach out to a school friend, as odd as she may be, or maybe the temptation to seek confirmation from a source that might be outside the accepted norm, is—"

"Carrie, this isn't about grief," my dad said with an irritated edge.

My mom recoiled at the rebuke.

Seeing them like this made my stomach knot up with tension. They'd argued before, but this was different. It felt more personal somehow.

"This is more of that . . . I don't even know what to call it," he said. "Acting out? Like the drinking and the lying?"

And getting your brother killed. He didn't say it aloud, but he didn't have to.

He is never going to forgive me. That thought rang in my head with stark clarity, like a bell that wouldn't stop reverberating.

"Micah, I think you're overreacting to—" my mom began.

"Don't." His hand shot up. "Stop defending him. You always defend him and that's how we ended up in this mess. You being too soft."

Mom reeled as if he'd slapped her. "I'm too . . . ," she gasped.

"There's nothing to defend. He knows better," my dad said.

"And you expect too much," she shot back.

"A little cooperation?" my dad snapped. "How is that too much?"

Mom laughed, a horrible grating noise. "A little

cooperation? Try total and uncompromising obedience. No mistakes allowed!" She swiped at her face, and I realized she was crying.

This was it, my family imploding in the middle of the kitchen, while grilled cheeses burned on the stove top.

"You're a fine one to lecture him about putting his needs first," she continued. "God forbid that the church ever take second place to us. To your *children*."

Dad pointed at her. "Oh, no. You knew exactly what you were getting into when we got married."

"Your commitment to the church, to God? Yes. I know all about that. But that doesn't undo your commitment to us. You made promises to *me*, too."

I don't know what scared me more: what my mom had just said or the fact that she'd said it so quietly.

Dad stared at her, his mouth thin and his breathing so harsh I could hear it.

"This church," he said after a long moment, "is also our family. If I fail and Riverwoods folds because of dwindling membership, there will be serious repercussions. Thirty-seven people work for the church in some capacity. This church is also what pays to keep the roof over your heads, food in your mouths, and college a possibility without a baseball scholarship."

That felt like a pointed finger jabbing into an open wound. I flinched.

"I'm the one responsible. I'm the one who is carrying the burden," he continued.

"Good to know that's how you see us," my mom said.

Oh. Shit.

Dad drew himself up to his full height, and I swear, I could see his nostrils flaring. "Carrie. You have no right to—"

"STOP!" The high-pitched shriek startled all of us.

My sister stood at the entrance to the kitchen, her small body shaking. She had Patsie in a stranglehold. "You're messing everything up! I put the cap back on the toothpaste every day. I make my bed." She sounded on the verge of hysterics. Her fingers plucked at the matted fur of Patsie's ear, removing tufts, and she didn't seem to realize it.

"Sarah." Frowning in concern, my dad took a couple of steps toward her.

"You have to stop yelling. You have to be good," she said in a trembling voice. "God killed Eli because I was bad, but I've done everything else I was supposed to!"

Oh, God. I looked over my shoulder to my parents for help, but my mom had her hand clamped over her mouth, tears running down her cheeks, and my dad seemed stunned.

He gathered himself enough to try again, bending down to Sarah's level. "Honey, come here and tell me—"

She bolted past him and tackled me around the knees.

I stumbled back under the force of her weight. "Sares." I tried to bend down to pick her up, but she locked her arms around my casted leg.

"I'm sorry. I said I was sorry, over and over again." She sobbed against my leg, her tears dampening my khakis and generally making me feel like the worst person alive. I touched the top of her head, which was overly warm and damp with sweat.

"Sarah, you didn't make anything bad happen to Eli," my dad said firmly.

The rest of his sentence—*Jace did*—hung unspoken in the air.

"What would ever make you think that, sweetie?" my mom asked.

"The last night," she said, barely able to catch her breath. "He was upset because I didn't put the cap on the toothpaste."

"I remember," I said quietly. I used to get in trouble with him for not turning the shampoo bottle upside down so it would be ready to squeeze. Weird how that had been absolutely infuriating at the time and now seemed kind of funny.

"It was just because I forgot. But he made me mad. So when he left the bathroom, I did something bad," she said, her voice muffled against my knee.

"What did you do?" I asked, mystified. What action could she have possibly taken that she'd feel responsible for Eli's death?

"I put his toothbrush back in the holder, but upside down, so it would be in the yucky water."

In spite of everything, the urge to laugh bubbled up.

"But God was watching, and he made Eli die to punish me. So I'd be sorry for being bad." She fell into silence, and any impulse I'd had to laugh dried up instantly. Her obsession with death had grown to the point where she seemed to be conflating God and Santa Claus into a single terrifying, all-seeing, punishing entity. I could kind of see it. She'd gone to bed that night before anything had happened. When she'd woken up in the morning, expecting to hear Eli spluttering in outrage, she'd been greeted instead by news of the accident from Delores, who'd been called in the middle of the night to watch her while my parents were at the hospital.

"You have to stop being mad," Sarah said, lifting her head to speak to my parents. "Or maybe God will kill Jace too to make you sorry." She sounded so solemn, so convinced of this inevitability, that it sent a chill through me.

My mouth worked, but words didn't come out at first. "Is that why you've been avoiding everyone?" I managed. "So you wouldn't mess up?"

She nodded, her cheek rubbing against the top of my

cast. It couldn't be comfortable, but she wasn't letting go.

I looked helplessly at my parents. My mom was sobbing softly, her shoulders shaking. My dad's face was stony and unreadable, but tears were gathering at the corners of his eyes.

He moved closer and bent down next to her, rubbing her back but making no attempt to pull her away. "Sarah, that's not how it works. God loves you. Elijah just went home." His voice broke, and he paused to collect himself. "God loves you. He wouldn't punish you like that. He doesn't punish anyone like that."

Sarah twisted around to look up at me, seeking confirmation.

I wanted to nod or say yes, but I couldn't make myself do it.

She gripped my leg tighter.

My dad glared at me. "I'll talk to God," he said to Sarah in a gentle voice, but that glare told me that our discussion about my defection to the daughter of the dark wasn't closed. "You know I've got a direct line to his ear. How about that?"

She turned her head toward him cautiously, sniffling. Then she nodded, and when he held out his hands, she lurched into them, crying again like her heart was breaking.

And it probably was. She blamed herself, and knowing

how blame worked, hearing the words "it's not your fault" wouldn't come close to touching the guilt.

I watched them go, my dad carrying her up the stairs and patting her back, humming a song so quietly I had to strain my ears to recognize it. "Jesus Loves Me."

Before the church grew so much and my mom quit working, she'd have to leave at night sometimes, to meet clients to go over paperwork or whatever, and if one of us had a nightmare, it was my dad who came in, bringing in the requisite glass of water or turning on the hallway light to prove that the shadow was only a shadow. He'd pat our backs like that and hum until we fell asleep again.

My vision blurred with tears.

My mom sighed and moved around me to follow them.

"Mom," I said. "I'm—"

"Not now, Jacob," she said, without looking back as she climbed the stairs.

The smoke alarm sounded a few seconds later, high and shrill, making me jump.

I moved to the stove to turn the burner off and then opened a window over the sink to let fresh air in.

Once the ringing stopped, I could hear the soft sound of voices upstairs. The three of them together, and me down here.

That's when I realized that even if missing Eli did get easier someday, even if the sharp edges softened with time as Thera had said they would, it wouldn't fix this. My family was broken, irretrievably. And even if my parents managed to hold it together for Sarah, I didn't fit in anymore.

I wasn't just missing the other half of myself.

I was alone.

CHAPTER FOURTEEN

THE WORDS IN FRONT of me on the page of *Gatsby* kept blurring. The Exempt study hall room was beyond warm again this morning, and my eyes were tired and dried out, like marbles rolled in sand.

The harsh but muffled voices of my parents fighting in their bedroom had continued late into the night. Then, once I'd finally fallen asleep, I'd promptly been sucked into an endless nightmare: I was stuck in a huge house with long, dark corridors of closed doors. And Eli was waiting for me, calling for me, but I couldn't find him, no matter how many doors I opened. The rooms were always empty.

I'd woken up this morning with my head throbbing and my shoulder muscles aching from the tension of my dream search.

My head, resting in my hand, slipped toward the desk, and it felt like too much effort to lift it. Maybe if I blinked really slowly this would work like a bunch of short naps.

"Jace."

I jerked, and looked up to see Mr. Sloane holding out a bright green hall pass. He frowned at me. "The library found the reference materials you were looking for, apparently." He glanced at the pass again. "Research for *Gatsby?*"

When I squinted at the pass Mr. Sloane was holding up, I was pretty sure the authorizing initials in the bottom corner were a large but messily scrawled *TC.*

Thera.

I'd been planning to find her today, to apologize again for kissing her. Even if I couldn't go over to her house anymore, I didn't want to lose the one person I could talk to because of a dumbass move on my part.

But maybe it wasn't so bad, not if she was sending passes to me in study hall to get me out.

It took me a minute to spot Thera across the library. She was on the far side of the oversized main desk, half hidden behind a computer monitor and talking to a senior I vaguely recognized, mainly from her hair. It was bright green and stuck out like a wing on one side and was shaved on the other.

Thera nodded in greeting as I approached the desk.

The senior turned and scowled at me, and the piercings in her eyebrows and the crease of her chin made her that much more imposing. "Get out of here, asshole."

I stopped.

"He's okay, Di," Thera said.

"You sure?"

"Yeah, thanks."

Di nodded, but the dyed side of hair didn't move. "I'll see you at lunch, T." Then she pushed back from the desk and walked away, taking deliberate care to jar my arm as she passed.

"She's friendly," I said to Thera once Di was gone.

"Don't take it personally," Thera said with a small smile. "She's not a big fan of the jocks at this school."

Is that what I was? Maybe once. But now?

"I wasn't sure you'd come." Thera's gaze flicked from my face to a point over my left shoulder.

"I wasn't sure you'd want me to," I said. "I thought maybe you might be mad after yesterday. I'm sorry if I—"

"Oh. No." Blushing, she dismissed my words with a wave, and then busied herself shuffling through a stack of papers on the desk. "I have something for you here somewhere." A page slid free and floated to the ground by my feet.

I bent down and scooped it up.

"'Fighting Eminent Domain Abuse: What You Need to

Know to Save Your Property,'" I said, reading the headline on the printout. "What's this?"

She studied me for a long second. "It's nothing," she said finally. "Not for you. Just a project I'm working on." She yanked the paper from my hand and stuffed it into an already messy stack. The top sheet was a printout of a search for local lawyers specializing in eminent domain, whatever that was, and beneath that, the edge of another article stuck out: GOVERNMENT SEIZURE OF PRIVATE PROPERTY: A SHORT HISTORY. Thera took her projects seriously, apparently. It all sounded boring to me.

"Here," she said, sliding a manila folder across to me. "This is for you."

"Gatsby" was scrawled across the front. "Really?" I asked.

She rolled her eyes at me. "Just open it, okay?"

I flipped it open. The first page was formatted text in tight paragraphs with a heading: NEAR DEATH, EXPLAINED. A few pages after that, TIME AND THE NEAR-DEATH EXPERIENCE.

The words made my skin prickle with unease. I looked up at her in question.

"It's some personal testimonies, a few articles and book excerpts, and summaries of a couple scientific studies I found online. Not many of those, though, because apparently it's a controversial area." Thera shrugged. "And some Wiki shit because that's practically unavoidable."

I waited.

She sighed. "Basically, it works out to this: only, like, ten to twenty percent of people who die and come back report any of the traditional 'symptoms' of an NDE."

I frowned. "ND what?"

"Near-death experience," she elaborated. "Didn't you do any research?"

No. Because I'd done my best to avoid even thinking about it.

"The bright light, chorus of angels, seeing dead family mem—" She winced, catching herself, and then continued. "The things you were expecting? They don't happen to everyone. No one knows why. There's a doctor who thinks it's got something to do with quantum physics, and your energy transitioning to a different state." Her voice warmed with excitement now that she was talking science again.

"Other people think it's because they were already in the process of coming back. Or maybe they don't remember what they saw," she said. "No one really knows for sure. There's a theory that near-death experiences aren't real, that they're the result of oxygen deprivation in the brain, but there's this neurologist who says that can't be it because the part of the brain that processes images and memories would already have shut down. . . ." She stopped herself, visibly reining in her enthusiasm, though seeing her that way—her cheeks flushed, her hands gesturing rapidly—only made me like her more. I knew that feeling of loving something so much, you wanted every word to convince others to join you.

"All I'm saying is you should check it out." Thera gestured toward the folder. "Just because you didn't see what you were expecting doesn't mean that there's nothing to see or that you saw nothing."

How many hours must she have spent gathering this information? And obviously not only printing it out but also reading it and trying to make sense of it for me?

I pictured her in her cozy room upstairs, surrounded by notes and textbooks, scrolling on a laptop for hours.

No one else could even stand to have me talk about it, but she'd done term-paper-level digging into the topic. For me—someone she barely knew and had no cause to help.

I closed the folder and picked it up. "Thank you," I said, my voice thick with emotion.

Thera flashed a smile that lit up her face. "You're welcome."

I stood there for a second, dazzled by her and wanting more. It was a strange, deep yearning that seemed to well up from the same place as the emptiness I normally felt. But I couldn't do anything about it, not after that impulsive but stupid kiss.

"So, okay, thanks," I said again lamely. I turned to go.

"Jace."

I faced her.

Thera hesitated, tucking her hair behind her ear. "About last night. You surprised me, that's all." She focused on the stapler, shifting it so that it would be perfectly parallel with the tape dispenser, pink rising in her pale skin. "But I was thinking, if you have time after school, there's this place I go sometimes when I need to clear my head." She raised her gaze, and I could read the vulnerability and uncertainty there. "We could go together."

A stupid grin threatened to spread across my face, and I wanted to shout, *Yes!* But suddenly, all I could think about was how many people might see us. Thera and me talking now, walking out after school together, getting in her rusted-out car with its distinctive patches of gray primer. And then, wherever this place was, if there were other people around . . .

Someone is always watching.

If my parents found out that I'd been seen with her again, I doubted any explanation would matter. Not after last night.

My silence stretched on for a fraction of a second too long, and Thera's expression shuttered. "You know what, never mind."

"Thera, no, I want to. But everything's really—"

"Complicated." Her cheeks turned a brick red. "Yeah. Like I said, forget it." She turned away from me.

"Wait." I reached over the edge of the desk and caught the sleeve of her hoodie. She seemed to have an endless supply of oversized hoodies.

She pulled free, focusing her attention on rearranging books on a cart.

"It's not like that," I said, trying to find the words to explain. "Someone saw me going to your house last night. And my family is going through some stuff right now. My dad thinks any kind of controversy . . ." I clamped my mouth shut, belatedly realizing I'd called her controversial.

"You don't need to explain," she said dully. "Trust me."

A catcall came from behind me, followed by a burst of laughter.

I looked over my shoulder to see Caleb and Matt at a table in the far corner. They were watching us. Or, rather, Thera. Matt had his chair tipped back on two legs and was grinning like an idiot, while Caleb waggled his tongue in the V between his index and middle finger.

Assholes.

As I turned to face Thera again, my mouth open to continue trying to explain, it dawned on me. That could have been me. No, that *would* have been me. If the accident hadn't happened, I would have been sitting right next to Matt and Caleb. Laughing.

And they knew nothing about Thera—the real Thera, the science nerd who covered her walls with the bridges she wanted to build, if she could ever get out of this town.

Not that they cared.

But I did. This new version of me did, anyway.

My dad didn't know Thera, nor did he want to know her. All that mattered to him was what other people thought of her and her mom, and I was beginning to think he felt the same about me and our family. What was left of it.

But Thera wasn't her mother, any more than I was my dad.

Plus, if I said no to Thera right now, I'd be walking away from the one person who'd helped me, who'd cared even though she was angry with me. And for what? For who? People who didn't care enough to bother knowing either of us or what we were struggling with.

Forget it.

I leaned on the desk, waiting until Thera looked up from the book cart. "Where do you want to meet?"

CHAPTER FIFTEEN

"SO WHERE ARE WE going exactly?" I asked Thera. The interior of her car was immaculate—not so much as a stray receipt or straw wrapper on the worn and stained gray mat beneath my feet. With the heater running full blast, it was warm in here and smelled of old dust, flowery air-freshener, and, faintly, her mint shampoo.

Thera grinned, keeping her focus on the road in front of her. "You'll see. You'll like it, I promise."

"Okay," I said. "But if we're making a run for the Canadian border, we're going to need more snacks." I held up the plastic baggie that had once contained a half dozen sugar cookies she'd evidently picked up at home. Now only a few small crumbs remained in one corner. She'd had one, and I'd demolished the rest. They were really good.

"Hmm." She pretended to consider that. "How do you feel about the Wisconsin border instead?"

I lowered the bag. "Seriously?"

I'd called my mom at lunch and told her that I was getting a ride home from Zach. Expecting a barrage of questions, I'd prepared an entire story about staying after school to work on Eli's memorial page for the yearbook, which was half true. The yearbook advisor, Mrs. Rafferty, had asked me about it on Monday, and it was something I would need to do eventually. But I didn't feel ready yet.

But when my mom answered, she'd sounded distracted.

"Okay, that's fine," she'd said once I'd finished explaining. "Just be home before dark, please." Then she'd hung up before I'd had a chance to reassure her that I would.

Her distraction was to my advantage today.

I watched as houses grew farther and farther apart and fields and horses took their place. Holy shit, maybe Thera wasn't kidding about the Wisconsin thing.

"So how do you know about this place, wherever it is?" I asked.

"Do you remember the hardware store that used to be on Main?" she asked. "A couple blocks from my house?"

"Sort of." My parents tended to go to the Home Depot on the other side of town. "It closed, right? Like years ago."

"That was my grandpa's."

"Yeah?"

She nodded. "He used to take me places with him, local vendors and random errands, during the summer, just to get me outside." She paused. "My mom doesn't really go out. Ever."

That wasn't news to me. There'd been rumors for years, ranging from ridiculously stupid to kind of plausible, about why that was. Psychic Mary was a werewolf. A serial killer. Horribly disfigured. Cursed. In a wheelchair.

But now it occurred to me there might be another reason. "Because of the whole psychic thing? Like she gets vibrations or . . ."

"Technically, she's a psychic medium, so it would be more like seeing ghosts, if it was anything." Thera shook her head, and I wasn't sure if it was a denial of the idea or of her mother's ability. "But it's not that, or at least, not just that," she said flatly.

Before I could decide if pushing further was wise, she pulled to the side of the road and parked in the ditch, next to an unmarked gravel entrance. A low metal gate blocked the opening, with a bent NO TRESPASSING sign in faded red and white hanging in the center.

"We're here," she said.

I had no idea where "here" was and whether our presence was allowed, but Thera was climbing out of the car.

By the time I'd gotten out and made my way up, she was waiting at the gate.

"Come on. They're closed for the day."

That was . . . reassuring?

She ducked under the metal gate with the ease and practice of someone who'd done it many times. I followed a little more awkwardly.

It was only a short walk up the dusty makeshift road to what was apparently our destination. And I stopped dead at the top of the incline at the sight of it.

Enormous mountains of loose rock and gravel ringed an open area below, where tire tracks marred the dusty surface. And with the sun low in the sky, the gravel and rock piles were turned into shadows limned in red and orange. It was alien and desolate, but also beautiful in a creepy way.

Thera kept going, walking down to the open area in the middle, where the wind whipped up small dust cyclones.

"What is this place?" I asked when I reached her.

"It's a quarry," she said, her hair flying out around her in the wind. "My grandpa used to buy landscaping materials from them." She pointed to a sign in the distance, a painted piece of plywood hanging crookedly on a metal pole: H&G GRAVEL AND SAND. "The main entrance and business office are on the other side. This is where the trucks pick up." She grinned at me. "It's weird, right?"

"Yeah," I admitted.

"It's best at sunrise and sunset," she said. "Like visiting the surface of Mars, you know?"

I couldn't argue with that. "But why? Why come here?"

She moved to stand next to me, so we were both staring out at the same strange vista. "Because sometimes it helps me to feel small," she said. "Reminds me that the world, the universe even, is a lot bigger than whatever shit is going on in my life at the moment." The back of her hand bumped mine; then her fingers curled against my palm loosely. "And that it won't be this bad forever." She sounded determined, tired, and sad, all at the same time.

I squeezed her hand gently.

"I read the papers you gave me. On the near-death experiences," I said.

Without letting go of my hand, she faced me. "Yeah? What did you think?"

"I don't know," I said. "Just because other people found a way to justify what they didn't see doesn't mean that they're right. Quantum theory or whatever. They're guessing."

"Yeah, but it doesn't mean they're wrong, either," Thera said.

"There's no proof." I tucked both of our hands in my pocket; her fingers were freezing.

She smiled at me. "Did you think there was going to be?" The wind caught her hair, whipping it across her mouth, until she was forced to reach up with her free hand and pull it away.

My gaze was drawn to the glimpse of pale skin beneath the corner of her jaw, at the curve of her neck. She revealed so little of herself. I caught myself imagining what it would be like to touch her there, one finger against that smooth, warm expanse. She was beautiful. And smart in unexpected ways.

"No one's going to convince you. For every argument on one side, there are equal and opposing ones on the other," Thera said.

"So what am I supposed to—"

"There aren't any easy answers. You have to figure it out." She nudged me with her elbow. "You know, think for yourself," she said with a smile that took the sting out of the words.

"I don't . . . I mean, I know how to think for myself." Except as soon as I said the words, I suddenly wasn't so sure. "This is different."

"Because you've always been told what to believe," she said matter-of-factly. "I was, too. Spirits, crystals, energies, all of that stuff." She flashed me a sad smile. "One of my earliest memories is of my mother burning sage in my room to make sure it was cleansed."

It had never occurred to me how similar we were, beneath the obvious differences. Her mother and my father both had enormous stakes in convincing the world that they knew what they were talking about.

"So what did you do?"

"I think you have to take the pieces that ring true to you, even if they don't all come from the same place. Sage smells pretty good, whether it works or not." She shrugged. "Loving your enemies as well as your friends is a pretty good one, even if it's tough to live up to sometimes. So is acknowledging that suffering is part of life." She grinned at me. "That's Buddhist, by the way."

Buddhism. I could see my dad's head exploding right now.

"For me, though, it's the big bang theory. A couple of years ago, they found evidence that suggests the universe is still expanding."

"Okay," I said slowly.

She laughed. "It's like ripples in a pond after you throw a rock in. It means something kicked off the start of the universe, something outside of the universe itself." She lifted her shoulder. "I don't think some old guy in robes was out there pushing dirt and rock into a ball to make planets, but that doesn't mean there's not a benevolent force out there somewhere. It seems pretty improbable that the universe came together randomly."

My head was spinning. "So we just pick what we believe. It's that simple."

"No, I don't think it's simple at all. And it's not just a single choice. I think as things happen, you have to keep choosing."

The weight of that seemed overwhelming and frightening. "You aren't supposed to choose, though. Are you? It's supposed to be . . ." I struggled to find the right words. "Like a lightning bolt. Saul by the side of the road or whatever. Or it's just something you have from the beginning." Active choice didn't play a role in any of the stories I knew, not like that.

"I mean, if a burning bush shows up and starts giving instructions, claiming to be God, then yeah, okay, maybe," I went on. "You have to decide if that's actually God or the result of using some serious drugs."

Thera snorted.

I shook my head. "But that's not the same thing as *deciding* to believe in God." It was such a foreign concept that I felt weird just saying the words.

"Choice matters," Thera said. "It defines us, more than what we're told to believe or told to do. If you believe that you'll see Eli again, in heaven or whatever comes after this, then believe that. Choose it."

I thought about the dream I'd had last night. It had felt so real. I could still hear that muffled murmur of Eli's voice behind those endless doors. He hadn't seemed gone, not then. "But what if I'm wrong?"

She lifted her shoulder in a shrug. "What if you are? You won't know it," she pointed out. "If you're wrong, then once you're gone, you're gone."

I shook my head. "I don't know if I can do that, just . . . choose." It seemed crazy that it was both that easy and complicated. It had been so much easier when I didn't have to think about it.

She edged closer. "Look, to believe in anything—God, other people, yourself—it's an act of defiance." Her expression was fierce. "We're small and fragile, and control relatively little of our existence." She waved a hand at the gravel mountains surrounding us. "Asteroids, cancer, sucky economy, someone cutting you off in traffic. The world will obliterate you as soon as look at you."

"That is . . . remarkably depressing."

"But we're here. We're alive against all those odds. And believing is a shout in the dark," Thera said, moving to stand directly in front of me. Her hand was tight on mine in my pocket. When she looked up at me, my breath caught in my throat and I went still.

She offered me a shaky smile, her gaze flicking between my eyes and my mouth. "And sometimes you have to shout."

I leaned forward to kiss her, letting go of her hand to sink my fingers into the warmth and heaviness of her hair.

When I teased her lower lip with my tongue, her mouth

opened beneath mine. I groaned, pulling her closer and mentally cursing my not-quite-functional left arm.

The heat and weight of her pressed against me, sending a heady rush through me. I hadn't felt this alive in months, and suddenly, I *needed* more. It was like I'd been living beneath a haze, a heavy coating covering me from head to toe, and it had been stripped away without notice.

My thumb traced her jawline and just below, exactly where I'd wanted to touch earlier, and she made a soft sound of pleasure against my mouth, tilting her head away so I'd have more access.

Thera fumbled with my coat, sliding her hands inside and around my waist, but my shirt rode up beneath her palms.

I sucked in a sharp breath. "So cold!"

She lurched back, clapping her hand over her mouth with a laugh. "Sorry!"

"It's okay." I moved to kiss her again, but instead she caught my hand and led me away, back over the hill and to the car.

Once inside, we were out of the wind, which helped.

The break and the silence in the car might have been awkward, self-consciousness catching up with us, except that Thera didn't let it.

She reached across the center console to trace the line

of the scar on my face with her fingertips, her expression troubled.

"It doesn't hurt," I said softly. "Not anymore."

Thera pressed her mouth gently across the end of the scar, near my cheek.

I squeezed my eyes shut, fighting the absurd urge to cry.

She pushed herself up on her knees and laid a series of soft kisses along the length of the scar.

I opened my eyes, moving my hands to her hips to steady her.

But that same *need* pressed down on me, and I slid my palm beneath her coat and the hem of her hoodie to the bare warm skin of her stomach.

The move was awkward and not nearly as smooth as it would have been if I'd been able to use my left hand, but that didn't seem to bother her.

She exhaled a shaky breath, air fluttering against my cheek. Then she grabbed my hand and tugged it past the soft satin of her bra to rest on her chest.

I looked up at her, and she nodded at me.

My fingers were beneath her bra strap, and I could feel the swell of her breast and the rapid thump of her heart against my palm. Like confirmation of life and being alive. The world hadn't gotten us yet.

Her mouth closed over mine again, and I was dizzy with the need to feel more—to feel her skin against mine in larger quantities, to feel alive in that unique way that came with ignoring the world to move together.

I tried to think, to speak. "Can we move to the back—" I began.

But headlights swept the interior then, and the rumble of a fast-approaching engine broke through our cocoon of isolation.

Thera pulled away, dropping back into her seat, and swiped at the fogged-over glass of the side window. A battered red pickup truck was pulling up alongside us. In the dim blue light of twilight, I could see the logo for H&G Gravel and Sand painted on the side.

"Shit," I said.

Thera scrambled for the keys in her jacket pocket. "Time to go."

"They're not closed for the day?" I asked.

"Apparently not today," she said with a sheepish grin, jabbing the keys in the ignition, starting up the engine, and pulling out onto the road.

I caught sight of an old guy hurriedly climbing out on the driver's side, his weathered and wrinkled face a mask of disapproval.

Twisting in my seat, I watched through the back window. The man took a few running steps toward us, his hand outstretched as if he would rap on the window or try to grab the door handle.

A spray of gravel flew up from Thera's rear tires as they finally caught the pavement, and he turned away to protect his face.

Then his foot seemed to catch on the edge of the road or something and he stumbled, falling down and hitting the ground. Hard.

CHAPTER SIXTEEN

"THERA." I TURNED TO face her.

"Crap." She bit her lip. "Yeah, I see," she said, her gaze flicking between the road ahead and her rearview mirror.

I glanced back. "He's not getting up." The old man's arms moved weakly by his sides, as if he was trying to push himself up, but that was it.

Thera slowed down and pulled to the side of the road, but she didn't shut off the car and made no move to get out. "If we go back and he calls the police . . ."

"Trespassing, yeah, I know," I said grimly. We'd probably be arrested. My parents would probably burst blood vessels.

"My mom can't come get me," Thera said, her voice barely a murmur above the roar of the heater. Not "won't" but "can't."

Which meant Thera would have to sit in jail until they decided to release her.

Not to mention, we'd both have criminal records, which would probably do fuck-all to help our chances with college admissions and scholarship committees next year.

But Thera didn't pull away. We sat there for a second, the engine idling loudly.

My gaze was glued to the man on the edge of the road behind us. I couldn't help picturing my brother, hanging upside down in the Jeep by the creek on Zach's family's property, waiting for someone to find him. It wasn't the same thing, I knew, and Eli had died almost instantly, or so everyone said. But I couldn't get that image of him out of my mind.

"I'll do it." The words burst out of me. "My parents are already mad at me anyway." With a shrug, I forced a laugh and shoved the door open.

"Jace . . . ," Thera said.

But I kept going. By the time I made my way back to the man and his truck, he was rolling into a sitting position on the asphalt with a dazed look. Blood trickled down from a bump on his forehead, and his chin was all scraped up. But he was conscious and didn't appear to be mortally wounded or anything.

Something that had been clenched tight in me relaxed

slightly. "Take it easy." I bent down awkwardly next to him, cursing my inability to move the way I used to. "I think maybe we should call an ambulance."

"Just got the wind knocked out of me," he said, glaring at me and dabbing at his forehead. Then he glanced at his fingertips and grimaced at the blood.

"I used to be a hell of a lot faster," he muttered. "I used to be a hell of a lot of things." He wiped his hand down the front of his worn denim shirt. "It's trespassing. You kids need to stay out of there." He jabbed a finger at someone or something behind me.

I glanced back to see Thera approaching warily, a first-aid kit in her hand. Of course she had one, probably kept in her perfectly organized and dust-free glove box.

"I've got it," I said to her. "You don't have to—"

"It's fine," she said to me.

Thera knelt on the other side of him and dug into the first-aid kit, pulling out bandages and a tube of anti-bacterial cream.

"Last year, we had a collapse when someone went climbing around in there," the old guy said. I was beginning to suspect he was either the H or G in H&G Gravel and Sand. "It's dangerous, that's why it's off-limits."

He pointed at Thera, and she stiffened. "You ought to know better," he said. Then he squinted at me.

Oh, crap, did he recognize me? It wasn't impossible. Riverwoods drew people from all over the Chicago suburbs and into Wisconsin.

"Both of you should know better," he added, but he didn't say anything more specific.

He allowed Thera to put a bandage on his chin, and he took the mini chemical cold-pack for his head, but he shrugged off her attempts to hand him the antibacterial cream.

"A few scrapes aren't going to make this mug any uglier." He pushed himself to his feet with a grunt and gingerly smoothed the stray wispy hairs on the top of his head. "Now, stay out." He gestured toward the gate and the quarry beyond. "Don't let me find you here again."

"Yes, sir," I mumbled automatically as I stood, grateful that calling the police seemed to be off the table.

Thera nodded, her dark hair falling over her face as she got to her feet and zipped up the first-aid kit.

I felt a pang of guilt that she'd lost one of the few places she seemed to enjoy.

"Or come back during business hours when someone else is here and can dig you out," he added grudgingly, eyeing her.

So he did know her, or at least recognized her.

"Okay," she said with a flash of that rare full smile.

He waved us off and started for his truck.

Thera nodded at me and we headed toward her car.

"And find someplace else to steam up the windows," the old guy shouted after us.

Thera made a choked sound, her cheeks flushing.

The absurdity of it all—getting caught fooling around by the side of a road in the middle of nowhere, at the entrance to a fucking quarry, in almost-Wisconsin; along with the now negated fear of getting arrested—suddenly registered with me. It was nothing I could have predicted or expected when I got up this morning. And that was a *good* feeling.

I laughed, almost light-headed with relief and something close to happiness.

CHAPTER SEVENTEEN

MY HOUSE LOOKED DARK and empty when Thera pulled to a stop about half a block away. The porch lights weren't on, and I couldn't see any sign of life inside.

I frowned.

"You're okay to walk this far?" Thera asked, her worried face illuminated by the yellowish light of the dashboard. "It might be icy now."

"Yeah, I'll be fine. I'm sorry that you can't pull into the—"

"No, no." Thera put her hands up in a protesting motion. "I don't want to be there any more than they would want me there, trust me."

"Thank you for . . . everything," I said, trying to make it as heartfelt as possible. I didn't have words for what she'd done for me today, this week.

A small smile played across her mouth. "You're welcome."

I leaned across the console and she turned to meet me halfway, but my mouth had barely touched hers before she pulled away.

"Back to reality," she said, nodding at the houses around us, her hair falling forward to hide her face.

I wanted to protest, but she had a fair point, unfortunately. "I'll see you tomorrow," I said, grabbing my backpack from the floor.

"Hey," Thera said as I pushed the door open, letting a rush of cold air inside.

"Yeah?" I paused.

"If this was just about needing someone to talk to while you figured things out, that's okay." Her words came out in a rush.

I cocked my head to the side.

She studied the steering wheel, rubbing her thumb along the edge of it. "I mean, you don't have to see me tomorrow. You don't have to do anything, it's not like we're—"

"I'll see you tomorrow," I said, grinning.

"All right." She ducked her head slightly with a pleased smile. "I'll send you a pass."

Thera's headlights lit my way on the uneven and slippery sidewalk, and she waited until I made it to our driveway before pulling away from the curb.

After fumbling for my key in my backpack, I managed to get the front door unlocked and open. As I walked inside and elbowed the door closed behind me, movement from the shadows in the living room made my heart catapult into my throat.

Sarah walked into the hallway, Patsie under her arm and a snack bowl in her hands.

"Jeez, Sarah, you scared me. What are you doing down here in the dark?" The lights were on in the kitchen, and blue flickers of the television came from the family room. "Where's Mom?"

She held a finger up to her mouth, her eyes big in the darkness.

I listened for a second and then I heard it. Voices upstairs, rising and falling, in an argument. My parents fighting, louder this time.

Tilting my head, I caught a few words.

". . . not my fault . . ."

". . . have to pay attention to what's going on around you, Micah! . . . needs help."

". . . other crises at the moment, in case you haven't noticed . . ."

Not good.

Sarah shifted her snack bowl to her other hand, caught my fingers, and then pulled me toward the kitchen.

"Did something else happen?" I whispered.

I expected her to shrug or just look at me, but instead she said, "Mrs. Percy showed one of my drawings to Mom, and she took me to the doctor. An emergency."

Mrs. Percy was her teacher. "A doctor?"

"Not the kind that gives you shots," Sarah added firmly, with the conviction that could only come from being told that exact information, word for word, multiple times. "I talked. And drew some more pictures."

A therapist. I couldn't believe Mom had actually done it.

"But Daddy's mad," she said in a small voice. "He came home early when Mommy told him."

Yeah, I bet. "He's not mad at you," I said. "He just feels bad that he couldn't help you."

Now that we were in the kitchen, I could see her more clearly, the red puffiness of her eyelids where she'd been crying, and . . .

I frowned. "Why is your face all orange?" Her mouth and cheeks were smeared with a sticky-looking orange dust and crumbs. "What are you eating?"

She smiled and held the bowl out. "I invented it. I was hungry."

I looked in the bowl to find cheese puffs and . . . Reese's Pieces? She must have been raiding deep in the cabinets to find my mom's secret stash of junk food. Which meant she'd been down here alone for a good while.

A mix of guilt and frustration made my chest pull tight. Sarah was too little to be caught up in all of this.

"That's disgusting, Sares," I said, keeping my tone light. I took a handful of her "invention" and tasted it to confirm, making an exaggerated face. "Yep, really gross."

She giggled. "No, it's not," she insisted. "It's good. It matches. See, orange and orange?" She rattled the bowl. "And the peanut butter and the cheese go together."

"Super gross," I said, ruffling her hair. "Good job. Come on, I know where Mom hides the emergency frozen pizzas."

"Can we have pepperoni?" she asked, surrendering the bowl to me.

"Sure, if there's one left." I put the bowl down on the island.

She hopped up on a breakfast stool and rested Patsie on the next one over while I shrugged out of my coat and dropped my backpack on the floor.

"Can I see what you drew?" I asked, once I had the oven preheating and the pizza on the pan.

She pointed to the manila folder on the other side of the island. It had her name written on the outside in careful teacher penmanship.

I flipped it open to find a series of crayon drawings on plain white paper.

The first one was pretty clear. Even if I hadn't recog-

earlier drawing stood on a cloud, beaming out at me. Light, as depicted by sharp yellow lines, radiated from his halo.

Eli.

I cleared my throat. "What's this one?" The picture looked normal compared to the others.

"The doctor who doesn't give shots"—clearly this was a big thing for Sarah—"told me to draw what I wished were true instead. I can't make Eli come back, though, so he had to stay in heaven."

"It's nice," I managed. She'd tried to give baseball back to me and our parents back to her. Everything about this drawing made me want to cry.

The oven beeped, and I turned away to open the door and slide the pizza in, keeping my back to Sarah until I got my shit together.

"She said it was okay," Sarah said. "She said it was okay that I was glad you're alive. She said Eli would understand, that he wouldn't be mad."

She didn't phrase it as a question, but I could hear her asking, nonetheless. And I didn't know what to say, at first.

Then I thought about everything Thera and I had been talking about the last couple of days. I didn't know what had happened to Eli, whether he was around or not, but I knew my brother. And I knew that if he were here, he wouldn't have wanted Sarah torturing herself this way.

So I made a choice.

"Yeah," I said. I turned to look at her so she'd see I meant it. "Eli would be all right with that. He wouldn't want you to be sad or hurting if you didn't have to be." I hesitated, then added, "You know he might have been upset about the toothbrush thing, if he'd found out, but he loved you, Sares. That's why he was hard on you sometimes, I think. He didn't mean to be, but he was trying to help."

I waited, expecting her to have more questions. But she was busy studying her orange fingers.

That was fine. It was better than before. She'd obviously been a little volcano about to burst from angst and despair. It had only taken the right prodding from someone outside the family to get her started on speaking up.

I handed her a napkin to wipe her fingers. If she'd gotten that crap on the white living room sofa, my mom was going to flip out.

"Is the pizza ready yet?" Sarah asked, scrubbing her hands.

A door slammed distantly upstairs.

Sarah and I eyed each other uneasily.

"Not a microwave," I reminded Sarah, trying to shift the conversation back. "The oven takes longer."

She heaved a sigh like I'd informed her she'd be eating asparagus and broccoli for dinner instead.

But it was so Sarah, so how Sarah used to be, that I had to smile. "Yeah, I know, life is tough. Come on, we'll go watch TV while we wait."

"*My Little Pony*?" she asked.

I groaned, but decided that in the name of distraction, I'd make the sacrifice. "One, that's it."

"Is your homework done?" she asked in a perfect imitation of my mom as she slid off the stool.

"Who's asking?" I demanded in mock seriousness.

"Me," she said.

"Then yes, absolutely."

"Mommy will check," Sarah warned, before scampering off for the family room sofa.

I looked up toward the ceiling and the heavy silence that seemed more ominous than the controlled shouting that had gone on before.

Yeah, I was pretty sure I was off the hook for a homework check tonight, no matter how much TV we watched.

CHAPTER EIGHTEEN

THE NEXT MORNING, MY pass from Thera arrived almost as soon as the bell rang for the start of Exempt. And I was ready, moving toward the front of the room before Mr. Sloane even called my name.

My palms were sweaty, but the rest of me felt light with anticipation and eagerness. I wanted yesterday all over again. I wanted that feeling of being less alone, but more specifically, I wanted that feeling of being connected to *her*.

I couldn't stop thinking about that moment in the car, her skin soft under my fingers and her breath in my ear.

When I walked into the library, Thera was reshelving books not far from the entrance. But I saw her before she saw me, so I had a moment just to look. She was scowling as she wrestled a stubborn book into place. Her dark hair was tucked in the back of her hoodie to keep it out of her way. But I knew what it looked like when it was loose and wild around her face. I knew what she looked like just before a kiss, her expression soft, her eyes half closed, her cheeks flushed with color. I *needed* that again.

"Hey," Thera said when I approached, her face lighting up, and I grinned in response.

But then her smile faded. "You look . . . Are you okay?"

I hadn't realized my sleepless night showed so much. "It's nothing."

Last night, my mom had made an appearance downstairs an hour or so after Sarah and I had eaten, her face white and her lips pinched. She'd said nothing about the frozen pizza or Sarah's lack of vegetables with said pizza. She'd just wrapped up the leftovers, loaded the dishwasher, told Sarah to get her pajamas on at eight, and then disappeared back upstairs, claiming a headache.

It was only when I heard the garage door going up a few minutes later that I realized my dad must have come down as well.

Sarah didn't notice Dad's departure, wrapped up as she was in her fourth episode of *My Little Pony*.

I let her stay up until nine, figuring it would be better if she was too tired to ask questions or notice that neither one of our parents was coming in to say good night.

My dad hadn't been home when I'd gone to my room

at ten thirty. So I'd left my door open, to listen. He'd rolled in close to midnight, as far as I could tell.

Not good.

"Family junk," I said to Thera.

Thera's forehead furrowed as she glanced from the book in her hand to me. "Did they say something to you about me dropping you off? I didn't think anyone was home."

"No," I said. "Nothing like that. They're fighting." I lowered my voice, years of training hard to break. "My mom took Sarah to a therapist and my dad's pissed. Dirty laundry or whatever."

"As if no one else has any," she said, rolling her eyes. "The stories I could tell you . . ."

I was sure she could. For all the fuss and drama around Psychic Mary from Riverwoods members, particularly from the conservatives in the congregation, the rest of town didn't seem to care as much. Cars came and went pretty regularly from her driveway.

"We're not allowed to," I said simply.

"Yeah. I get it." She bobbed her head, keeping her focus on the shelf in front of her. I wanted to move closer, but she seemed more distant today. Maybe it was being at school, or maybe it was because she was working.

Or maybe she'd decided yesterday was a mistake.

The thought made me feel a little shaky. I leaned

against the next shelf over to take the weight off my leg. "So, I was thinking, you took me to one of your favorite places yesterday, maybe I could return the favor this afternoon." I'd planned it out last night, while I was lying awake.

But Thera hesitated, avoiding my gaze.

My heart sank. "What's wrong?"

She shook her head. "It's nothing."

Except it clearly was. "Did someone say something to you?"

"No. It's fine." Thera waved my concern away and then slid another book in place with a solid *thunk.*

I didn't quite believe her, but she obviously didn't want to talk about it. After a moment, she took a deep breath, pushing away whatever was bothering her, and turned in my direction. "So," she said with a smile. "What did you have in mind for this afternoon?"

I grinned. "How do you feel about drive-ins?"

She blinked at me. "Like the movies?"

"Nope, like the food. There's this place in Richmond, Dog 'N' Suds. My friends make fun of me, but it's one of my favorite places to go. Hot dogs and root beer in glass mugs and they bring it to your car and everything."

Thera raised her eyebrows. "Like . . . a drive-through?" she asked, in a tone of mock astonishment.

"Shhhh!"

The annoyed voice came from somewhere behind us, and it was immediately followed by a fit of giggles.

Thera rolled her eyes, and then, with a quick look back at the main desk, she abandoned her cart and took my hand, pulling me across the library.

She led me down an aisle that ended in a small alcove full of old reference books, like encyclopedias. I didn't know they made those anymore.

"You want to go to a drive-in," she said with skepticism. "Didn't those go out of business in, like, the seventies?"

"Okay, now I'm seeing why you kept our destination yesterday a secret. 'Hey, Jace, want to go stare at a bunch of rocks with me?'"

She laughed.

"But I was on board, and it was good. And this will be too, promise." It was hard to describe what I loved about Dog 'N' Suds. Something about the feeling of being warm and enclosed in the car, with greasy but good food eaten together instead of devoured straight from the paper bag while on the way to somewhere else. It felt like a special occasion, an event instead of just another meal. Before the church really took off, when my parents didn't have much money, they used to take Eli and me there on our birthday.

I stepped closer and tucked Thera's hair, wild as usual, behind her ear. "Are you in?"

She tilted her chin up until her mouth was almost touching mine. "Yes," she whispered, and I flashed back to those minutes in her car yesterday, her smooth skin and the rapid but steady tremor of her heartbeat under my fingertips.

God, this girl.

"But only if you promise they'll roller-skate my food to me," she added in that same husky whisper, her lips brushing mine. "I can't tolerate anything less."

"Smart-ass," I said with a smile. "I think they walk it out to you in the winter."

Thera sighed in pretend disappointment. "I suppose that's acceptable." She wrapped her arms around my neck and kissed me, open-mouthed and unself-conscious, and it took all I had not to press her back against the shelves.

The loud sound of someone clearing their throat obnoxiously a few moments later made us jump apart.

Mrs. Paulson stood at the entrance to the alcove, her arms folded over her chest. "You have students waiting at the desk, Thera," she said. But her stern expression seemed at odds with the amusement glinting in her eyes.

"Sorry," Thera said quickly, and moved away from me to join Mrs. Paulson, who was already turning toward the front of the library. At the last second, Thera glanced over her shoulder, her cheeks flushed pink, and mouthed, *Busted.*

But then she grinned at me.

Yeah, everything was going to be okay.

CHAPTER NINETEEN

AT LUNCH, I FOUND myself staring at the big clock on the far wall that was ticking off the minutes way too slowly.

Just a few hours to go. I could feel a dopey smile pulling at my face and I didn't care.

"What is going on with you?" Zach asked.

"Huh?" I glanced at him next to me.

"It's just, you're different." He waved a hand at me in a vague gesture. "Suddenly you're, like, . . . up. I don't know."

"Things are better today." Instead of feeling like my limbs weighed a thousand pounds each, I could move, I could breathe.

"Because of her," Zach said.

I went still. "What?"

Zach made an impatient noise. "Dude, I saw you

getting in her car after school yesterday. Caleb saw you talking to her in the library. And in the hallway," he said, and paused expectantly, waiting for an explanation.

"Caleb needs to mind his own business." And keep his hands to himself.

Farther down the table, Caleb looked up from his nachos. "What's up?"

"Psycho Mary's daughter," Zach said.

"Nothing," I said at the same time.

"Bro." Caleb shook his head, a smear of bright orange cheese in the corner of his mouth. "I'm all for a little fun, but you're taking it too far. People saw you."

"Shut the fuck up," I snapped. Now the entire table was staring at me.

"What are you doing?" Zach leaned closer.

I turned to face him. "You don't know her, and you need to stop talking. Now."

His eyes widened at the not-so-subtle threat in my tone. "Wait, you're not sleeping with her, are you? Because that is—"

I shoved his shoulder, hard enough for him to get that I meant it. "Shut it. I'm serious."

Zach raked his hand through his hair. "I can't believe you're doing this to us."

"Us?"

"Your friends. Me. The team," he said, gesturing to all

the faces now watching avidly. "You're the one who said she was trouble, that she liked to cause problems for fun and—"

"That bitch cost us state last year," Scott called from the other end of the table.

I glared at him. "We had it wrong, okay? She's not like that." I'd never asked her about Doug and Aaron, but I knew her—and the situation—well enough now that I could guess what had happened and what hadn't. She was not the type of person to lie about harassment or worse, which meant Doug and Aaron had done exactly what she'd accused them of. They'd just figured they wouldn't get caught, or that even if they did, no one would believe her because of who she was. The worst part was, they were right. Most people didn't believe Thera. Or at least not entirely.

Scott snorted. "Yeah."

"Wait." Caleb stared at me in disbelief. "You're not, like, serious about this, are you?" He shook his head. "That girl has more miles on her than—"

I launched myself across the table. His tray went flying as I reached for him, fists swinging, and suddenly, everyone was shouting.

"What the fuck, dude?" Caleb half fell, half slid out of his chair, pressing his hand against his nose.

Zach yanked me back. I struggled to pull free from him.

"All right, all right!" Derek stood, leaning over the table. "Enough."

Caleb got to his feet, glaring death at me as blood seeped between his fingers, and I shook Zack off me.

"The thing is, you're still a member of the team, Palmer," Derek said. "You're on the roster."

I stiffened. "So?"

"So, you know better than anyone that we need a good year," Derek continued, sounding uneasy but resolute. "If she's aiming for another crack at us, you're giving her the perfect opportunity."

It took me a second to understand. Derek didn't care if the rumors were true; none of them did. It was enough that whispers existed. They weren't willing to take the chance, so he was saying I had to choose.

My temper flared again. "Then take me off," I said. I felt loss like a huge hole through my middle as soon as I said the words, but also a little relief at making a decision, picking a direction and taking action. If I was going to move forward, maybe that meant breaking with what was left of my old life.

"What?" Zach and Derek said it at the same time, with identical expressions of shock.

"I'm not playing. I'm not going to play again. I can't. So take me off." I grabbed my tray of food—or what was left of it—from the table.

"But you can't!" Zach protested.

"You're worried about it, I'm giving you a solution," I said. Weirdly enough, I could hear my dad in the cold snap of my words.

"You're choosing her over the team?" Derek asked. "That's low, dude."

I turned to him. "I don't have a team anymore. I can't *play*." Juggling my tray with my good hand, I held up my left arm, which was still bent at the elbow. "In case you missed it, my life took a giant fucking left turn when I least expected. So, yeah, maybe I'm not making decisions you agree with, but I don't have the same choices I did before. *I'm* not the same as before. I have to learn to live with it. You do too."

"But—" Zach began.

I faced him. "And Thera is not your problem. She's not a problem at all. Leave her alone. Leave *us* alone."

They stared at me like I'd announced my decision to transfer to Parkland and play for them. Actually, worse than that. Like I'd announced my decision to play soccer instead.

Disgusted, I shook my head and walked away.

But after about a dozen steps, I realized I wasn't entirely sure where I was going.

Obviously, eating at the team table wasn't a good idea. Surveying the cafeteria, I felt the first pinch of doubt. In cutting ties to my teammates, I'd pretty much cut ties to all my friends as well.

Whatever. I'd be fine. I would just go to the library. Thera had class, but I had plenty of other things to do, including looking at memorial pages in previous yearbooks to get ideas for Eli's.

Shifting directions, I collided with someone coming the other way.

"Sorry," I said, stumbling back, trying to keep my grip on my tray.

"It's all right," Kylie said, her dark ponytail swaying. "I think I owe you one in this department." She bent down to scoop up the carton of milk that had tumbled to the floor, and handed it back to me. "See you," she said, ducking my gaze.

Then she walked away without another word. No apologies, no pleas to talk. It was like we were strangers again.

"Hey," I called after her. "Is everything okay?"

She stopped, surprised. "I didn't think you were talking to me."

I grimaced. "I . . . yeah. Sorry about that." At the moment, I couldn't quite recall why it had been necessary to cut her off so completely after we broke up. It seemed like eons ago.

I blew out a breath. "I was stupid. Hurt, I guess." But that was before I knew what it was like to really lose someone for good.

Kylie nodded, her fingers fidgeting with her meal card. "It's okay." She hesitated. "They're giving you crap?" She tipped her head back toward the table where Zach, Derek, and Caleb were arguing.

I frowned. "How did you . . . ?" Of course. She would have heard about it because of Scott or from Scott directly. "Yeah, they don't like me hanging out with Thera. Catoulus," I added, as if there was another Thera. "Psychic Mary's daughter." I was daring her to react. We used to be friends before the mess last year. Her opinion still mattered to me; otherwise it probably wouldn't have hurt so much when she dumped me for Dylan.

But she just studied her meal card, as if the information or photo on it were new to her. "Are you happy?"

"It's only been a couple days since we started talking," I said carefully, "but I'm . . . better than I was." I hesitated, then added, "She's amazing."

"Then who cares what they think?" she asked with a shrug. "Sometimes there's only one choice, even if nobody else likes it. If they're really your friends, they'll get over it."

I'd never thought about the crap she must have gotten from her brother or from everyone else on the team when she ended things. Shit. I'd really screwed that up.

"I'll see you later." Kylie touched my shoulder lightly and then moved past me.

"Hey."

She turned back.

"I really am sorry about before. When we broke up, I mean. I was a tool. I didn't know. I didn't get it." I lifted my shoulders helplessly. "I was feeling what I was feeling, and I didn't think about you." I'd never really had the experience of going against everyone else to do what I thought was right. So I'd failed to recognize the effort it must have taken her to do it.

She nodded slowly. "I could have handled it better, not sprung it on you like that," she said. "That's all I've ever wanted to tell you. I kind of freaked because it was, like, all the pieces of my life kept getting tangled tighter and tighter. We were friends and then we weren't because we were more and then there was another tie to the team—always the team—and you're my brother's friend. . . ."

"Maybe not anymore," I pointed out.

"Eh." She rolled her eyes. "You can do better."

I laughed.

"Just be careful with her, okay?"

"They're rumors, Kylie. She's not—"

"Not like that." She waved her hand dismissively. "I meant how you treat her."

I straightened up. "What? Why?"

"You put people on a pedestal sometimes and then get pissed when they mess up and fall off."

"I'm the last person to judge someone for being a screwup," I said, forcing a laugh.

"Exactly my point," she said gently. "You're so busy seeing yourself as less than, you don't see it in anyone else until it's too late. Until they've disappointed you or hurt you, and then you cut them off. It's kind of all-or-nothing with you. Not everybody can live up to that."

That sounded a little too familiar, like something I'd thought about my dad. "It's not like that," I said quickly. "*I'm* not like that."

"Yeah? We were friends for six years before we got together, and you've spent the last six months pretending I don't exist."

"But that was because—"

"How long will it be before you talk to Derek again?" Kylie jerked her head toward the table where they'd settled, without me. "Or Zach?"

"They were—"

"Expressing an opinion other than what you thought was right?" she asked.

I clamped my mouth shut.

"It's none of my business, obviously," she said with an uneasy smile. "I'm not sure what we are anymore. Not friends, not really. But I want you to be happy, and I don't want you to be hurt again when someone else can't be what you think they're supposed to be."

Before I could respond, someone called her name from the line behind me.

She waved in response. "I gotta go," she said to me. Then with a last careful pat on my shoulder, she was gone.

I turned to watch her rejoin her friends in line.

And at the table that used to be mine, my friends were watching too. They'd evidently caught the interaction between Kylie and me.

Zach waved me over.

But I was still pissed. I headed toward the doors to the hall instead.

Kylie was wrong. It wasn't about expecting people to be perfect. That was my dad, not me. I was just tired of being blindsided all the time.

CHAPTER TWENTY

THERA INSISTED ON PICKING me up in the turnaround at the front of the school.

"I could have walked to the car," I told her as I pulled the passenger door open, wincing at the squeal of the hinges.

"And what if someone needs to track down our roller-skating waitress this afternoon?" she asked in a mock-serious tone. "I need you to be well rested."

"Hi," I said with a grin as I dropped into the seat. I'd been looking forward to this all day.

"Hi." Her mouth curved into a welcoming smile.

Unable to resist, I leaned over the center console and kissed her. She opened her mouth beneath mine, making me groan, and her fingers, chilled from the air, slid around the back of my neck, sending a pleasant shiver through me.

I pulled back a little. "You know, we don't have to go right away," I murmured against her ear. "We could just—"

A car honked behind us. "Let's go, Romeo," some-one's dad shouted.

Thera laughed, and I sighed.

I slipped out of my backpack and dropped it on the floor, where it landed with a thud that shook the whole car, and then I shut my door.

"What do you have in there?" She frowned in the direction of my bag. "Weights?"

"I met with Mrs. Rafferty after English," I said, pulling my seat belt on. "She gave me some old yearbooks to look through."

"For Eli's page?" Thera navigated her boat of a car carefully through the crowd of people.

"Yeah." I'd skimmed the memorial pages in the selected volumes—at least that way what I'd told my mom I was doing after school wasn't a complete fabrication. Some of the memorial pages were as much as ten years old. The hairstyles and clothes of the memorialized were frozen permanently in that time period. Their smiles beaming out from the page because they didn't know they were going to die. They didn't know that they wouldn't ever have kids or grow old or be bitter or happy. They were just gone. Leaving behind a page of black-and-white photos that seemed wholly inadequate. And the longer they'd been dead, the worse it felt to look at their pages, thinking of all the things they'd missed out on. All the things Eli would miss.

"I'm sure whatever you pick will be perfect," Thera said.

"It's not that. Not exactly. I don't want this"—I nudged my backpack and the yearbooks inside with my foot—"to be what people think of when they think of Eli. I don't want this to be his future."

She didn't say anything, the blinker clicking quietly in the silence as we made the turn to go north to Richmond.

"It's just, six months ago, I knew what my life was going to be. What our lives were going to be. I'd get a baseball scholarship somewhere warm. Florida. Arizona. Eli would probably stick pretty close to home and Riverwoods. Wheaton, maybe. I couldn't wait to get out of here, but not because of him, not like that. I just wanted a chance to be me. Instead of Jace-and-Eli. Or Pastor Palmer's kid." I stared out the side window, watching the buildings pass by without really seeing them. "It would have been the first time we were apart for any real length of time, you know? But I knew we would be back together. On weekends or Christmas or whatever. We were different, but he was . . . the other half of me." I lifted my shoulders helplessly. "Sometimes I feel so off balance, like the whole right side of my body is missing and I'm trying to move without it. I don't know what to picture for my life, how to see a future that doesn't have him in it."

How could I imagine a future in which Eli did not have one, where he was a photo I might pull up on my phone when people asked if I had siblings? How do you explain that you're a twin when you're not anymore?

"It's like someone told you to build something but took away all your materials at the last second," Thera said. "And now you're not even sure if you want to try with what little you've got left."

I straightened up in my seat and stared at her. "Exactly." But the knowing tone in her voice was more than empathy; it was experience.

"What about you?" I asked. "Big plans for engineering college or something?" I had no idea what kind of classes or training engineers were required to have.

"It's complicated," she said, keeping her gaze focused on the road ahead.

The same word Eli and I had both used to describe our family; I was positive that wasn't a coincidence.

I shrugged. "I'm not going anywhere. I was promised hot dogs and root beer in a frosted mug."

"Processed meat and frozen glassware? That's all it takes with you?" she asked with a teasing smile, but it contained a hint of weariness.

"Processed meat with chili," I corrected. "And yeah."

She rolled her eyes. "Fine."

But she didn't say anything for a long moment.

"My mom is all I have. We're on our own. My dad has never been around. Never met the guy and don't particularly want to." Thera didn't sound angry, just matter-of-fact.

"But my mom has this kind of messed-up view of the world. She doesn't care about what happens out here, it's all about the higher power of the universe and the messages she says she gets." Thera's hands fluttered up from the wheel in a dramatic gesture that I presumed was meant to be an imitation of her mother. "Sometimes I think she's hiding behind that because she doesn't want to deal with reality."

"Reality like . . . ," I prompted.

"Paying bills," Thera said in exasperation. "Keeping enough food in the pantry or the right kind. Making sure she doesn't hurt herself. Dealing with the city when they send their letters about our grass being too long or when they try to take—" She cut herself off with a jerk of her head. "Reality for me is, I can't leave her here by herself." Her words sounded flat and empty, like this was something she'd recited to herself over and over again at night, as if repetition would make it more palatable. "Sometimes I can't even be gone for school the whole day before she needs me."

I wanted to ask why, what was wrong with Mary, because

that was definitely the implication, but the tension in Thera's arms and shoulders told me it was a no-go area.

"So even assuming I can get into one of the good engineering schools, U of I or Purdue, maybe, and get scholarships, there's just no way." Thera took a deep breath. "My future is at McHenry County College, taking, like, bookkeeping classes or something. Something that will get me a job in an office instead of behind a fryer."

"That's not right," I burst out.

She smiled faintly. "Thanks."

I shifted in my seat to face her. "No, I'm serious. There has to be something else you can do." She was basically a hostage to her mother's choices. I knew all about that. No matter where I went or what I did, I would always be Pastor Palmer's kid when I was here, captive to standards I had no choice in.

"I appreciate the thought, but like I said, it's complicated," Thera said, in a tone that suggested the end of the conversation.

"But that's such a waste," I said. If I'd learned anything from the accident, it was that life was perilously short. Too short to not do something she obviously loved as much as those bridges on her walls. "And it's not fair to you."

Her mouth tightened into something closer to a grimace. "There's not much room for fair in the equation when it comes to family."

Which you already know. I could hear the words even though she didn't say them.

"But, Thera, you have to—"

"I don't want to talk about it anymore," she said sharply.

"Okay," I said, holding my hands up in surrender. "Sorry."

"It's not . . ." She took another of those breaths that seemed to fill her from her head to her worn combat boots. "This is supposed to be fun. I want to have fun. Please?" she pleaded.

I wondered how little of it—fun—she was having if she was carrying that much responsibility at home and trying to stay ahead at school.

"Sure," I said.

Her hand left the wheel and fumbled for my palm, and then she threaded her fingers through mine.

A few minutes passed like that, with the roar of the heater, the quiet and staticky murmur of the radio, and her fingertips cool against my skin.

"So I looked up some stuff last night," I said. "Big bang theory, God, near-death experiences, resurrection."

"Some light reading, then." She glanced over at me.

"Yeah," I said with a laugh. I hesitated, then added, "I keep trying to put all the pieces together, but I can't make everything fit. Like, if there's nothing after this life, if it's just that blackness I saw"—it was still hard for me to say that aloud, even to Thera—"then what about Jesus coming back after dying? I mean, that's the core belief in our religion. Did somebody just make it all up?"

"And?"

I shook my head. "There are some who say that it's because everyone believed in magic then, not science, so they were fooled by whatever the resurrection 'witnesses' said. But then there are arguments that people back then were way more sophisticated than we give them credit for, and the first Christians died horribly for their beliefs, so they had to have seen something to convince them to suffer that way. Plus, apparently, if you were picking witnesses to convince everyone of a resurrection that didn't happen, you wouldn't have chosen women because no one respected them then. And—" I stopped, realizing I was talking faster and faster.

Thera grinned at me.

"It's interesting," I admitted. "Stuff I never thought about before."

"Told you," she said simply.

I lifted our joined hands and kissed the back of her wrist. "Are you sure you don't want to pull over somewhere?" Something about her just made me thirsty—for her time, her thoughts, and yeah, okay, her body.

She laughed. "We're so close now," she said, tipping

her head toward the windshield. "You want to tell me what I'm looking for?"

"There." I pointed to the red roof of Dog 'N' Suds, visible now on the left side of the road. There really wasn't much to the structure—the small enclosed area where the food was prepared, and the long roof that extended over the spaces where people could park and order. A big cartoon dog—the offspring of Snoopy and Goofy, seemingly—adorned a matching red sign out front.

"Oh, it's kind of cute," she said in surprise as we drew closer. She let go of my hand to reclaim the steering wheel before she hit the turn signal.

"You were expecting . . ."

"I don't know, something old and kind of falling down, I guess. But this is better," she said, sounding intrigued as she made the turn into the parking lot.

"Just because they were popular in the fifties or whatever doesn't mean they were all built then," I pointed out.

"Fair enough," she said.

"'Oh ye of little faith,'" I added with a grin. It was one of the few Bible quotes I could remember, though given the old-timey language, I was pretty sure it was something my grandfather used to say all the time rather than something from one of my dad's sermons.

"Ha," Thera said drily. "Yeah. That's me. So, what do I do?"

"Pull into one of the spaces with a menu board. Unless you'd rather order at the window and eat outside." I pointed at the picnic benches that lined the edge of the parking area.

She looked at me, aghast. "It's, like, thirty-five degrees outside!"

"Yeah, well, I didn't know if it was okay to eat in here. I'm pretty sure you must vacuum this car every day for it to be this clean." I pretended to look around.

"It's only every other day," Thera said with a half smile. "Otherwise, the neighbors complain about the noise of the vacuum outside."

I laughed, though I wasn't sure if she was totally kidding. Considering one of her neighbors was Riverwoods, where some people were looking for any excuse to hate on Thera and her mother, I wouldn't doubt it.

"All right, so now what?" she asked, pulling into an open space and putting the car in park. We were one of three cars under the roof. The cold had kept everyone else away apparently.

"We look at the menu and decide," I said. "Then when we're ready, we press the button to tell the waitress to come over."

"A drive-through is more efficient," Thera said, wrinkling her nose.

"It's not about efficiency," I protested. "It's about atmosphere."

Thera laughed. "Well, clearly. I mean, who wouldn't go out of their way to eat in this car?"

"You wait, you'll see." Then I added, "And I'm pretty glad to be eating here."

"Yeah?" She leaned a little closer to me.

"It's not just the car, but the company," I said, reaching out to brush my thumb across her cheek.

"Hmm. Maybe you're onto something there," she said, turning her face into my touch.

But when I moved in to kiss her, she pulled back. "Oh, no. We're on a mission."

I groaned.

With an amused sound, she turned to consult the menu. "All right, let's check out our options. I'm guessing you're going to recommend the chili dog and root beer?"

"Technically, it's a Coney Dog, and yes, if your soul isn't dead," I responded immediately, and then winced at my choice of words. *Nice, Jace.* But for a second, I'd forgotten. About Eli, about everything.

Thera didn't seem to notice. "How about my taste buds?" she asked with faux seriousness. "What if they're in mortal peril?"

"Please tell me you're not a vegan."

"Nope, I'm just particular about my choices." She glanced back at me with a smile, and her gaze caught mine and held.

"Yeah, I noticed," I said softly, the blood thundering in my head already.

Thera shifted in her seat to face me, and this time, she leaned over and brushed her mouth over mine, warm and soft.

I touched my tongue to her lips, and they parted, welcoming me. She tasted of cinnamon gum, and I wanted more.

She wrapped her hands around the back of my neck to pull me closer. I sucked her lower lip into my mouth, running my tongue over the edge of it, and she made a soft sound that electrified me and made me want to pull her over the console into my lap.

The rap on her window made us both jump and jump apart, and my first thought was that the waitress had gotten annoyed with us taking so long to order or someone had complained about us kissing.

But when I looked out the window behind Thera, it wasn't a shivering waitress in a red-and-yellow uniform shirt, but a familiar figure in a green-and-white letterman's jacket. He was leaning with his hands braced on the roof of Thera's car, his face looming at the edge of the window frame.

"Caleb," I said in disbelief. His nose was a little puffy from the blow I'd landed at lunch.

Thera stiffened and threw a glance over her shoulder.

"What's going on? What are you doing here?" I asked, loud enough for my words to carry through the glass.

Thera reached reluctantly for the window buttons.

"No, don't," I said to her. I didn't want him to have any more access to her than he already had.

"Let's go. Come on." Even with the barrier between us, his harsh tone came through loud and clear. He rapped loudly on the window again, for no reason at all, beyond seeing Thera jolt.

"I'll be right back," I said to Thera grimly, reaching behind me for the door handle. I didn't want to take my eyes off him.

"This isn't a good idea. We can leave," Thera said. "Go somewhere else." She sounded both tired and alarmed.

"No, we were here first." This was my place, not his. Which brought another disturbing question to mind.

I got out of the car and slammed the door shut. "What the hell? Did you follow us?" I asked Caleb. I couldn't imagine the odds of him just happening to end up here. I should have known he'd be pissed about what happened at lunch. "What is wrong with you?"

He came around the back end of the car to get in my face. "You're choosing that over us?" he demanded,

flinging a hand in Thera's general direction.

Some of it was about Thera, but I bet it was also partly that I'd embarrassed him at lunch. Caleb could dish shit, but he couldn't take it.

My temper flared, and I struggled to keep a handle on it. "I'm not on the team anymore, and she has nothing to do with you or them. Just forget it, okay?"

He gave a derisive laugh. "Dude, she's got your dick so twisted in a knot you can't see straight."

"Shut up," I snapped.

"She's a tease, everyone knows that. And you're a fucking idiot if you fall for it. She just wants the attention to—"

I lashed out, sending my fist flying toward his face. Unfortunately, it was my left, which meant the punch didn't carry nearly the impact it would have before the accident and surgeries.

Caleb stumbled back for a second, surprised; then his face turned a deep shade of red, the veins in his forehead popping to prominence. "Oh, you are a punk-ass bitch."

It spiraled quickly from there. He lunged forward and took me to the ground, and the adrenaline sang in my veins, so hitting the hard concrete of the parking pad didn't even hurt.

But I felt his knuckles connect with my nose and the lightning zap of pain that made my head spin and the corresponding gush of hot blood.

That pissed me off. I shoved up, and we went over in the other direction, me on top of him, landing punches wherever I could.

That cycle repeated a couple more times, each of us taking the advantage of leverage and trying to use it to pound the crap out of the other.

Someone screamed, and glass crashed. A tray, most likely. A tiny, distant part of my brain mourned the loss of all that food and root beer.

"911! Call 911!" someone shouted.

"Stop! Get in the car now," Thera said, yanking backward on the collar of my coat until I stumbled to my feet.

"You're her little bitch now?" Caleb asked, rolling to a sitting position before spitting blood. His teeth were pink with it.

I lunged toward him, my heartbeat pounding like a drum in my ears.

But Thera stepped between us.

"Not unless you want to be in the back of a squad car," she hissed at me, her hand flat on my chest.

It took me a second to process what she meant. Then, in the distance, I heard the growing wail of sirens.

Fighting in a public place. That would definitely get back to my dad if the cops caught us and made it official.

I nodded at Thera and she lowered her hand. We started toward her car.

"That's right, run like a little pussy," Caleb shouted after me.

I tensed.

"Let's go." Thera opened the passenger-side door and pushed me toward the opening.

I flipped Caleb the finger—see if he thought it was so funny this time—and got in.

And when I shut the door, in the side-view mirror I saw Matt and Corey, our right fielder, scrambling out of Caleb's car to pull him off the ground.

Good. I hadn't been as outmatched as I'd felt. I smiled, and pain, emerging from the blanket of adrenaline, ricocheted between all the hot spots on my face.

My gaze shifted to my own reflection in the mirror.

Blood dripped steadily out of my swollen nose; I could taste it, coppery and sour in my mouth, now that I was paying attention. My right eye was puffy and bruised-looking already, and there was a gash beneath my left that was adding to the blood flow.

"Shit." I looked like a Halloween mask. And the ache in my previously injured left arm and leg was sharpening with every second that passed. I had really pushed myself too far this time.

"Yeah, that's pretty much what I thought too," Thera said as she pulled away from Dog 'N' Suds.

"I can't go home like this," I said, feeling a surge of panic. "Sarah will freak. She's got this obsession with death and dying. If I show up—"

"First, let's get the bleeding stopped," Thera said, not even flinching as the police cars sped past us in the opposite direction. "I think you left about half of your blood in the parking lot. There should be napkins in the glove box."

I opened it and grabbed a handful of them, leaving bloody fingerprints all over everything. "Sorry," I muttered.

"And there might be some gauze left in the first-aid kit. I didn't have a chance to replace the Band-Aids yet."

I bent forward to look for the kit, trying to keep the blood from dripping all over her car, and tentatively applied the napkins to my nose. It had been so long since I'd been punched in the face, I'd forgotten how much it hurt. My eyes were watering from the pain, which upgraded to agony the second I touched my face.

"You know, it would be nice if we could go somewhere once without someone needing medical attention," Thera said as I fumbled for the gauze inside the kit.

"Twice is a pattern?" I asked, my voice muffled.

"It seems like more than a coincidence," she said. "You didn't need to do that, you know. I'm used to Caleb and a lot worse. I can handle it."

"You shouldn't have to." I pushed the gauze into my nose. Not a great look, but it would help.

"Defending my honor, were you?" she asked in an acid tone that told me there was definitely a wrong answer to that question.

"No, shutting him up was all about him. He's an asshole." The car took a pothole, jostling my hand against my nose. "Ow, damn it," I said through my teeth. "And I used to be more like him than I'd like to remember."

"But what good does it do? He's going to have that much more to prove the next time he sees either one of us," Thera pointed out.

"He'll think twice about it first, that's the good it does," I snapped.

"Too bad you bought that good with your face. I think that cut under your eye might need stitches."

I shook my head and regretted it immediately when the pain roared to new heights. "No, no way. If we go to the ER, they'll call my parents. If we just butterfly it, I can tell them I slipped in the hall or—"

"I don't have any butterfly bandages, Jace," she said.

"I think I saw a CVS on the way here. . . ."

She gave a disbelieving laugh. "That's not going to fix this." Her hand moved in a gesture that encompassed the mess that was presumably me.

I looked down at myself, at the blood and dirt in smears

all over my coat and jeans. My shirt, under my open coat, was worse in terms of blood splatter.

"Shit," I muttered again.

Thera sighed. "I have an idea." She did not sound happy about it. "We have butterfly bandages at my house, I think. And one of those stain stick things. We could go there, get you cleaned up."

It was a solid plan, one that solved the problem, but from her tone, you'd think she'd suggested turning ourselves in at the police station and getting first aid from them.

"You don't have to worry," I said. "I won't say anything about what you told me earlier. About your mom, I mean." That was the only reason I could think of for her uncertainty. I'd been to her house before, after all.

Her mouth settled into a thin, tight line as she changed lanes. "I know. *You'll* be fine."

CHAPTER TWENTY-ONE

THERA PARKED IN THE credit union lot behind her house. Pulling into her driveway wasn't an option, with Riverwoods' original building directly across the street. Any number of people might see me as they went in or out on church business, and in my current condition— gauze up my nose, bloodstains everywhere, and a fast-food napkin plastered against the cut under my eye—I was definitely eye-catching.

The back of Thera's house looked a little worse than the front. The paint was peeling, and a couple of the windows were fogged from broken seals. A sad-looking chain-link fence, rusted and sagging, encircled the microscopic backyard, and the grass was thin and patchy. Dead vines and leaves clung to the fence, and random bits of litter, most of them ATM receipts from the credit union, were entangled at the base. The only thing that looked new was the prominent yellow-and-black sign stabbed into the frozen ground between the end of her yard and the start of the credit union parking lot.

The headline—NOTICE OF PUBLIC HEARING—screamed in all caps, but the details beneath were in such small letters that I could barely make out a date and time set for next month.

And the sign apparently didn't only *look* new. When Thera saw it, she slowed, her shoulders hunched as she took it in.

"What's that about?" I asked.

"Nothing," she said. "More city council bullshit." She took off then, toward a side door, at a faster clip than I could manage.

Thera stopped on a set of sagging wooden steps by the side door to wait for me to catch up. "My mom is probably with a phone client, and I don't want to disturb her," she said as I approached. "So we're going straight upstairs to the bathroom."

Her eyes wouldn't meet mine, her gaze flicking from my face to some unknown point over my shoulder.

"Okay," I said. She didn't want me to meet her mother for some reason. I was almost sure of it now.

Thera opened the door and stepped up onto the worn black-and-white linoleum floor of their kitchen. I followed.

She moved swiftly past a closed wooden swinging door and then veered left through an open doorway, which turned out to be the hallway I'd been in the other night.

With an urgent look, Thera waved at me to hurry up as she rounded the newel post and started up the stairs.

"Thera?" The soft female voice came through the closed pocket doors behind me.

Thera froze, one foot on the second step, dismay written all over her face.

But she tried to rally. "Yeah, it's me," she said, in a voice that sounded almost normal, as she gave me a panicked look and held her finger to her lips. "I'm back."

A long pause followed. "With who?"

Thera's head dropped, her shoulders curving forward in defeat.

What was going on here?

"With Jace Palmer," she said finally, reluctance rounding and slowing her words, like they were a hard candy she didn't want to spit out.

"I'm finished for the day," her mother called. "You should both come in."

"We're kind of in the middle of something, Mom."

"I would like to meet him." Mary's voice was light, but the demand beneath it was steel, unmissable and unbendable. "And I'm sure he would like to meet me. Wouldn't you, Mr. Palmer?"

I jolted at being addressed directly and at the assurance in her tone. She was right, though I hadn't really thought about it until that second.

Thera rolled her eyes. "That impresses you?" she asked in a whisper, leaning over the railing to speak to me.

"She knew I was here," I argued.

"No, she knew *someone* was here," Thera said. "Because she heard footsteps."

"But she knew I wanted to meet her."

Thera gave me a tired look. "Everyone always wants to meet her."

Then she drew in a deep breath, as if accepting a terrible fate that could no longer be fought, and descended the stairs to stand with me in the foyer.

"I like you," she said, her gaze searching my face, as if seeking reassurance or answers I didn't have.

"I like you too," I said, confused. It was a strange moment for an out-of-the-blue confession of something I already knew.

"But if you hurt her, Palmer, no matter what she says, I'll make sure you hurt too. Got it?" She edged past me, heading toward the closed pocket doors.

Uh, okay. Frowning, I turned to follow. "Why would I—"

"People see her as an easy target."

"Because of what she does?" I asked.

She rubbed her forehead, as if a headache was forming.

"Sometimes. But sometimes it's because people are jerks."

Well, I couldn't really argue with that logic.

I moved out of the way, feeling my nerves kick in for the first time. I had no idea what to expect, meeting Psychic Mary. She was practically a mythical figure in my house and this town, often mentioned but never seen.

I would just keep my mouth shut. That couldn't hurt anything.

Thera pushed the wooden doors into the pockets in the walls on either side and led the way in. Her face as she walked in was one of someone anticipating a punch, which I didn't understand at all.

I followed cautiously. The room, like the rest of the house, was clean but old. Faded wallpaper and rugs, the furniture and built-in bookshelves made of dark, heavy wood that looked like something my grandparents would have had before they moved to Florida. A familiar-looking carved cross, polished to a dull gleam, hung in a central position on the opposite wall between the windows.

A modern, oversized sofa dominated one side of the room, with a wooden table and chairs pushed up in front of it. Mary, Thera's mother, sat in the center of the couch.

Her similarity to Thera was immediately apparent. She had the same dark, wild curls, though Mary had hers braided neatly and hanging over her shoulder.

The rest, though . . .

I looked away quickly so my shock wouldn't register with her. The temptation to stare was almost overwhelming, but I could also sense the strain in Thera, standing a few feet away, waiting for my reaction.

Mary was . . . I didn't know the right word for it. "Large" didn't seem close to adequate. Her eyes, cheekbones, and chin were nearly lost in bubbles of excess flesh. Her dress was a voluminous swath of fabric, more like a sheet, white with tiny delicate purple flowers. I wasn't sure if she'd be able to walk. A wheelchair folded up discreetly in the far corner of the room suggested that I might be right about that.

People are jerks. Thera's words echoed suddenly in my head. This was what she'd meant. Not the psychic thing, or not only that, anyway.

"Oh, my God! Thera, what happened?" Mary stared at my face, aghast.

"There was an incident—" Thera began.

"Here, Jacob, come and sit here." Mary pushed a wooden chair out toward me with a puffy bare foot. The ease with which she did it suggested lots of practice. Her toenails were painted a shiny purple color.

But I didn't move. Thera was slightly in front of me, blocking my path, and she didn't seem inclined to step out of the way. And going around her felt wrong, given the sudden tension throbbing in the room.

"Thera, go and get the first-aid kit," Mary said. "It's upstairs."

Thera stared at her mother, her jaw tight. "I know where it is."

"We might have some of those butterfly bandages left," Mary added, her eyes focused on my face.

"Do you think so?" Thera asked sharply.

And finally Mary glanced from me to her daughter. They engaged in a long second of silent conversation, before Thera made a frustrated noise.

"Fine. I'll be right back." But instead of retreating, Thera charged forward and pulled a worn spiral notebook off the couch next to her mother. I hadn't noticed it before.

Mary sighed. "Thera . . ."

But Thera ignored her and pushed past me back out into the hall. A moment later, her footsteps pounded up the stairs like she was in a race.

"Come on." Mary waved me forward. "You look like you're about ready to fall over."

I edged toward the chair and sat down cautiously. Even still, a groan escaped. All my muscles were tightening up.

"What happened?" Mary asked, leaning forward slightly.

I wasn't sure where to look. I didn't want to stare at her, but completely avoiding looking in her direction seemed wrong too. "I fell." Might as well try the story I hoped to sell to my parents.

Mary snorted, a noise very similar to the one her daughter made at times, and the movement made her whole body shake. "Onto someone's fists?"

I laughed reluctantly, and my ribs protested. "Ow." I pressed my palm against my side and realized for the first time I'd split the skin over my knuckles as well.

Mary sucked in a breath in a sympathetic hiss. "What happened?" she asked again.

Caleb. Dude had a hard head. Or, more specifically, a hard face. "It was stupid. Somebody was running his mouth, and I—"

"Here." Thera reentered the room, breathless, with a box of bandages and a first-aid kit that was a twin to the one in her car.

She set both on the table and started to pull out another chair.

But Mary stopped her. "Ice pack?" she asked, looking toward Thera, as if she expected Thera to produce it from behind her back.

"Mom—" Thera protested.

"Without it, the boy's nose is going to blow up to twice its size," Mary said pointedly.

I didn't understand what was going on here, but I was definitely missing something.

Thera exhaled loudly and turned to go through the swinging door into the kitchen. The slam of the freezer door sounded a moment later.

"You should take that gauze out now," Mary said, pulling tissues from the box on the table and laying them out on the wooden surface. "If you wait, the blood will coagulate around the gauze and your nose will bleed all over again when the gauze comes out."

I stared at her.

She lifted her shoulders in a small shrug. "I started nursing school. A long time ago."

Wincing, I pulled the gauze from my nose and crumpled it up into the tissues she'd laid out.

Mary handed me another tissue for the small trickle of blood that ran out of my nose. It was nothing like the gushing of before.

The noisy crash of ice cubes hitting the counter came from the kitchen.

"And grab some of the bath salts Cecilia left the last time she was over here," Mary called, before turning to me. "She and I trade services. She owns the spa a couple of blocks over. If you soak in the salts tonight, that should help with some of the soreness."

"Oh. Okay." I hadn't taken a bath since I was, like, seven, but I might be willing to try it if it would help.

Thera returned with a baggie of ice cubes wrapped in

a small towel, and a clear plastic box with what appeared to be tiny crystals, handing both to me. "Anything else?" she asked her mother, almost daring her.

"No, that should be everything," Mary said, seemingly unconcerned. "Let's see your face, Jacob."

I put the ice pack and crystals down on the table and peeled back the stuck napkin with a grimace.

Mary shifted forward, as if she might try to stand to help, but then she sank back into the sofa weakly. "Thera," she said, out of breath.

"Yeah, I got it." Thera dragged a chair around and positioned herself to the side of me.

"Did you—" Mary started.

"Yes, I washed my hands," Thera said without glancing in her direction. "So what I'm going to do," she said to me, "is kind of pinch together the sides of the cut and use the bandage to hold them in place. It's probably going to pull a little."

That did not sound like fun, but it was better than stitches at the ER. "Okay."

She pulled the backing off the first bandage and leaned in, both hands coming straight at my eye.

I automatically moved back.

She shook her head with a smile. "You're going to flinch on me, aren't you?"

"Nope. I'm totally okay with you putting your fingers in my eye."

"I thought sports guys were supposed to be tough," she said with a laugh.

"Not a sports guy anymore," I pointed out.

She touched my cheek gently with her thumb, away from all my injuries. It was soothing rather than clinical, for a different kind of hurt.

Out of the corner of my eye—the one Thera was not currently endangering—I saw Mary watching us, her head cocked to the side with curiosity.

I shut my eyes then, and with quick, almost professional efficiency, Thera applied three butterfly bandages. She had done this before.

"There. That should help," she said.

I opened my eyes and she handed me the ice bag in the towel for my nose. "But be careful not to get the bandages wet. Cover them with a bigger bandage when you get home."

Home. I looked down at myself. I wasn't actively bleeding anymore, but I was kind of a mess. Part two of the problem.

Thera looked me up and down speculatively. "If we clean the worst spots on your jeans and coat and if you zip your coat up over your shirt—"

"—I might be able to get to my room to change without sending Sarah into a panic," I said with a nod. "As long as she doesn't see my face first."

"I can loan you one of my hoodies." Thera shrugged. "Might be a little short on you, but it'll work for that purpose. They're men's anyway."

I smiled. "Thanks."

She smiled back. "You're welcome."

"Thera, why don't you take his coat to the laundry room? You might need to soak some of those spots."

I straightened up, slightly alarmed. I was keeping my pants, no matter how professional and clinical they were about this.

Thera snorted, guessing the direction of my thoughts. "We have more than one stain stick."

But she made no immediate move to leave the room. Instead, she and her mother had one of those quick, silent conversations, before Thera shook her head and disappeared through the swinging door into the kitchen.

She returned in a few seconds with a bright orange plastic tube and handed it to me, after I shrugged painfully out of my coat.

Thera took it, and with one last warning look at her mother that I didn't understand, she left the room again.

"Was the fight about Thera?" Mary asked quietly as I tugged at the cap on the tube.

I hesitated, not sure of the dynamic here and whether I should answer.

"I know she has a hard time still sometimes," Mary

continued. "But she won't talk about it, not with me." A tear trickled down her cheek, and she wiped it away. "Last year was horrible for her. I really thought I might lose her."

"The fight wasn't about Thera," I said quickly, not sure what to do with that information or Mary's emotional reaction. Thera seemed like the last person who would consider hurting herself. "Not like that. It was more about me and my friends. My former friends, I guess." I focused on applying the stain stick to the largest of the bloodstains on the legs of my jeans. "Some of them don't like how things have changed with me. After the accident. After—"

"After Eli," Mary supplied.

"Yeah," I said. "They were blaming Thera for the changes, and I made sure they knew that it wasn't her fault."

"If the other guy looks anything like you do, I suspect you made your point," Mary said wryly.

"Good," I said with grim satisfaction.

"Thank you for being kind to her."

I glanced up, surprised. "It's not about that. I mean, I'm not . . . being kind. She's . . ." My face went hot. "I like her," I mumbled. This was not the type of thing you talk about with parents. Particularly not the parent of the girl whose tongue was in your mouth not that long ago.

"I've always found her rather likable myself," Mary said, her eyes sparkling with humor now instead of tears.

"Yeah," I said, uncomfortable. I scrubbed harder at the splotch, starting to see some difference beyond making a wet patch on my jeans.

"Give me your hand," Mary said.

I froze. "What?"

She held up the tube of antibacterial cream from the first-aid kit. "You should get those knuckles cleaned up."

"Oh." Relief washed over me.

"Did you think I was going to read your palm?" she asked, amused.

"No, I . . ."

"I'm not a palmist. Contrary to the sign in the window," she said. It seemed like years ago, instead of a couple of days, that I'd felt it beckoning me across the street.

"I got a good deal on it. eBay," she said with a grin that made her look a lot younger. I could see even more of Thera in her at that moment.

I put the stain stick down on the table and scooted to the edge of my seat, holding my hand out to her, a bit wary.

Mary took it, her fingers soft and light on the edges of my hand, and rested my palm on the table in front of her. "I'm glad you came with Thera today," she said, pulling out a couple of Band-Aids from the kit. "I wanted a chance to convey my sympathies in person." She smiled tentatively. "I don't think I've spoken to you since you and

Eli were little boys chasing each other in the churchyard with sticks and making laser sounds."

I had no memory of ever speaking to her, but she was right about the sticks. "We weren't allowed to have toy guns or swords. Lightsabers even," I said, more to myself than to her.

She opened the antibacterial cream and began dabbing it gently over the worst of my split skin.

"Elijah was a good friend to Thera," Mary said. "I know she misses him terribly."

I blinked back unshed tears. Both for the loss of my brother and for the idea that he'd felt he had to hide his friendship with Thera from me.

"Yeah," I said. "I miss him too."

Mary unwrapped one of the bandages and peeled the backing off. "You know, your grandfather used to come over here."

"He did?"

She nodded at the wooden cross on the wall. "Gave me that."

No wonder it looked so familiar. He used to carve in his spare time. We had one of his crosses in the dining room at my house.

"He was trying to save us, I think. But I never had the heart to tell him that I'm Catholic, born and raised." She winked at me.

Huh. My formerly Lutheran grandfather probably would have looked on that as almost equally suspect.

She was quiet for a long moment, sticking the edges of the bandage carefully over my knuckle. "You know what I do here?" she asked. "My responsibility?"

Inexplicably, my pulse accelerated, either with dread or anticipation. I couldn't tell which. "Yes. I mean, a little, I guess."

"Sometimes the ones who've passed visit me," she said as she removed another bandage from its packaging. "They can see me, like a light in the darkness."

The darkness. For a second it was difficult to breathe, remembering the thick, smothering blackness I'd experienced.

"It's dark for them?" I managed, sounding choked.

"Temporarily, before they move on to their final place, yes, it seems to be." Mary lined up the second bandage over my hand.

"So you can't just talk to anyone who's . . . passed?" I asked.

"Only if they want to be reached, but the easiest ones are those who are newly passed and have a strong desire to communicate. A message." Mary looked up at me, her dark eyes telling me what I needed to ask, my role in this play.

"Everything okay in there?" Thera's voice drifted

through the closed swinging door, but neither of us responded.

I wasn't sure if I believed Mary, but my insides were shaking suddenly, like we'd taken this conversation onto a pitted and potholed road. I had to follow through. I had to know.

"Did you hear from Eli?" The words escaped in a rush, and I flinched at hearing them aloud.

But Mary didn't so much as pause. "Thera has my notebook, so I don't have exact wording. But he wanted you to know he was okay. He knew you were blaming yourself, and he didn't want you to do that. It was an accident, and that's all. It was not your fault."

The shaking in me increased, only this time it felt like relief, the rush of collapsing adrenaline. "Really?" In spite of my doubts, hearing those words, that Eli didn't blame me, worked on me. I couldn't stop tears from welling in my eyes.

Mary nodded, squeezing my fingertips gently.

I wanted to sag back in my chair, but I was still balanced on the edge, my hand on the table, with Mary's hand covering it.

"But he did have a message for you," she said.

My wariness returned, and I straightened in my chair. "What's that?"

"He wants you to finish what he started." Her forehead

crinkled in concentration, as if trying to recall the exact wording. "He showed me a folder or papers or something. It wasn't clear."

"Showed you?" I asked. "How would he show you? I don't understand—"

"Mom! Stop it!" Thera stood in the doorway, my dripping coat in her hand and a stricken expression on her face.

But Mary tightened her fingers over mine. "I think he wants you to help us."

CHAPTER TWENTY-TWO

THERA CHARGED INTO THE room, my coat clutched in her fist. "I told you, he doesn't know anything about it. Leave him alone!"

"Help you how?" I asked Mary.

But Mary's attention was focused on her daughter. "Thera, you know I have an obligation to the—"

"Oh, screw the universe and your messages!" Thera shouted at her, her breathing ragged.

"Thera, what's wrong?" I asked, pulling my hand away from Mary's.

"Thera, sweetie," Mary said patiently. "I'm sorry but—"

"You're not sorry, you're never sorry." Thera's voice was shrill.

I stood and went to Thera. "Hey, hey, it's okay." I pulled her close, but she was stiff and unyielding. "Whatever it is—"

"I tried to stop her, I didn't want her to say anything to you," Thera said. "That's why I took her notebook."

"His brother wants him to know. He deserves to know," Mary said.

"Deserves to know what?" I had the feeling I wasn't going to like the answer when I finally got it.

"Can we just go?" Thera pleaded. "We'll just leave now and forget it." She pushed my coat at me.

I took a step back from her. "Why can't you just tell me?" Dread was gathering in the pit of my stomach.

"Thera," Mary prompted, but her daughter ignored her. *Please?* Thera mouthed at me.

I shook my head. Thera's shoulders slumped and she moved away from me, folding her arms across her middle.

"The message from Eli is real," Mary began. "Before the accident, he was trying to—"

"I'll do it," Thera said, glaring at her mother. She put my coat carefully on the back of a chair, but she didn't say anything for a long moment. "What I told you was true," she said finally. "Eli was my tutor and he did come over here, so I wouldn't have to spend any more time away from my mom."

I could hear the "but" hanging in the air between us.

"Even then, I guess he already knew about the first offer from Riverwoods for our house. Probably from your dad, or maybe from the work you guys were doing at the church. I mean, you guys own everything else on the block already anyway." I blinked, processing that information slowly, too slowly.

The expansion? That's what this was about? I tried to formulate a thought or a coherent question. "What does that have to do with—"

Then, it clicked. The coffeehouse, parking structure, bookstore, and whatever else depicted on those detailed drawings—they all had to go somewhere.

Apparently, right where I was standing.

How had I missed that?

Honestly, it had never occurred to me to look at the drawings that closely. I'd assumed that they would be building down by the auditorium instead.

"Oh, my God, I'm so sorry. I had no idea they were pressuring you guys to sell again." I frowned. "Wait. Are you saying Eli had something to do with—"

She shook her head. "Eli never brought it up, but after we told Riverwoods no, he was here when we got the first notice from the city council that they would be taking our land for 'public good.'"

"They can't do that," I said automatically. But the image of that sign about the public hearing, newly posted in her yard, immediately flipped to the front of my mind.

"They can," Thera said with weary certainty. "It's called eminent domain."

The term sounded familiar, and it took me a second to figure out why: the papers she'd had in the library the other day. She'd been doing research on it.

"They say they need our land to expand the road," Thera said. "But that also happens to leave plenty of room for a parking garage built and maintained by the city." Her mouth thinned into a bitter-looking line.

And on the weekends, Riverwoods members would have the parking they were always complaining about, right next to all the new buildings they would have donated money for. Now I could see it. Crap.

"We can't leave here," Mary said. "We don't have anywhere else to go. This house was my parents'. It's paid for. The money they're offering is not enough for us to buy anything else."

And Mary, who was clearly not well and never left the house, would be forced to move.

"Eli was trying to help us," Thera said. "He thought he had a way to stop the expansion." She frowned. "He'd found something he thought would make it all go away."

I stared at her, as if she'd just announced that Eli had decided to shave his head and join a cult. "He would never do that. Riverwoods was his life." But more than that, he would never go against my dad. Eli was the "good" one.

"He can, he did," Thera said.

"I don't believe you," I said, an unsettled, panicky

feeling rising in me. Eli might have tried to help in some way—finding them another place to live or organizing a fund-raiser because he and Leah lived for that crap—but Eli and my dad were the same. Riverwoods always came first.

She flinched, but refused to acknowledge my words. "That last night, he was supposed to bring me whatever he'd found, so we could take it to a lawyer and try to stop the process before it got started. But—"

"He came here for that?" I *knew* he'd been lying about where he was that night.

Thera nodded. "A couple of hours before the accident." She paused. "I was with him when he got your call asking for a ride."

Suddenly that weird conversation—our last—in the Jeep made sense, Eli talking about right and wrong and hurting people.

My head felt loose and disconnected, like it was bobbing above my shoulders on a string. Thera actually might not be lying. But Eli had never said a word to me about any of it, unless you counted a random, hypothetical conversation. I didn't.

How was that possible? Something so huge and he'd never mentioned it to me? The idea made me feel like I was falling again, being tossed and tumbled in the Jeep, before being thrown free.

I'd told him everything—okay, more than anyone else. I didn't think we kept secrets of this size. It made him into someone I didn't know, literally a stranger with my face. And now he was gone, making it impossible to push for answers or explanations.

"If that's true, then what's all this about 'finishing what he started and helping us'?" I asked, waving my hand in Mary's direction. "You got what you wanted."

"He changed his mind," Thera said softly. "He came to tell me in person that he had to hold on to whatever he'd found. He couldn't give it to me. I was hoping he'd change his mind—"

"But then he died," I said.

"Yeah." She dropped into the nearest chair and rested her head in her hands, her fingers tangling in her hair.

"I'm so sorry, Jace," Mary said. "I wouldn't have brought it up if Eli hadn't come through so clearly to me."

Thera sighed. "Mom."

But I wasn't really listening. Because in that moment, a horribly simple idea dawned on me, one that sent a wave of devastation through me. "Is that what all of this was about?"

Thera looked up. "What?"

I cleared my throat. "You, me, the quarry, everything. Was it really about this? Your house, the church."

"No. Of course not!" Thera shot to her feet.

But she'd hesitated just a fraction of a second before answering. That was an answer, in and of itself. I mean, how could she *not* have considered it? So many people thought of Eli and me as interchangeable. Make me care, make me trust her, and then ask me for a tiny favor. Or better yet, one day I'd invite her over when my parents weren't home, and she'd have the chance to look for whatever she thought Eli had.

It was only logical.

I waited silently.

After a moment, Thera shifted her weight from foot to foot, her gaze dropping to the floor. "At the very beginning, okay, yes, I thought about it. I wondered if Eli had told you, if you might know, but when it was clear that you didn't, I *let it go*. And then I got to know you." Her expression softened. "You weren't what I thought. You were like me, trying to figure stuff out. And what happened between us was real." She raised her chin defiantly, daring me to contradict her.

"Then why not tell me about all of this?" That was the part that really stuck with me, like a knife between my shoulder blades.

She threw her hands up in frustration. "Because you were so lost! You could barely handle Eli being gone. What do you think would have happened if I'd told you?"

To be fair, she sort of had a point. And yet, it didn't change a damn thing. I'd spent the last two months trying to pull myself out of a dark hole of guilt and grief and confusion, and I'd finally found a few footholds this week because of her. But now it was like none of that mattered. I couldn't trust her, so the footholds were gone and I was back at the bottom of that pit again.

"I gotta go." I grabbed my coat off the chair and turned away from her, shoving my arms through the sleeves.

"Jacob," Mary began as I walked out of the room.

"Wait, Jace, please." Thera followed me to the front door. "Your coat is wet. You'll freeze."

"I'll be fine." I yanked at the front door, but it wouldn't budge.

Thera moved to stand in front of me. "You can't walk home from here, it's too far." She touched my arm, and I jerked away. "Let me get my keys and I'll—"

"I can't deal with this right now," I said, avoiding her gaze. "Not from you."

Thera sucked in a sharp, pained breath, and then there was nothing but a heavy silence.

After a moment, she reached out and undid the dead bolt with a loud snap, then moved out of my way.

And I left.

CHAPTER TWENTY-THREE

MY MOM GASPED WHEN I opened the door to the minivan and climbed in. "You said you were a little banged up! That is not a little!" She'd pulled to the curb around the corner from the old sanctuary and Psychic Mary's to pick me up.

"Your face is purple and red," Sarah said from her booster seat in the second row. "What happened to you?" She sounded worried, but not too panicked.

"I'm fine," I said as calmly as I could, dropping onto the front passenger seat and shutting the door. "It was my own stupid fault. I took the stairs faster than I should have and wiped out. Can we go home now? Please?" I pulled on my seat belt. I just wanted to be gone.

But instead, my mom reached out and touched my chin, turning my face toward her, her forehead furrowed with concern. "I still think the school should have called me. Do you need to go to the emergency room?"

"No, it's not as bad as it looks. And it was after school, no one was there. Someone patched me up with a first-aid kit from their car." That, at least, was partially true.

Mom made a disbelieving noise as she finally—*finally*—put the van in gear and pulled away from the curb. "And Zachary couldn't give you a ride all the way home because . . ."

"I told him he could drop me off here," I said as I held my hands against the heater vents to warm them, repeating the lie I'd given her on the phone. My coat, zipped all the way up to cover my shirt, was frosty with cold in the wet places that had started to freeze. "He had to get back to practice. They're doing strength training in the gym this week, I guess."

Pained sympathy flashed across my mom's face, and I felt like an even bigger jerk. "I'm sorry, I know you must miss it," she said.

"Yeah," was all I could say. Because I wasn't sure if I did, at least not in the way she meant. What I think I actually missed most was the certainty it gave me, of knowing my place in the world. Without it and without Eli—or at least the Eli I thought I knew—I was adrift.

"But you should have gone into the church, at least," Mom said with a frown. "Waited inside where it was warm."

I noticed that she wasn't asking why I hadn't walked

the additional block or so to ask my dad for a ride home, though he was probably at the office. "Didn't feel like dealing with people and all the questions."

To my surprise, Mom simply nodded in understanding instead of lecturing me about my responsibilities or maintaining a good face—even when my literal one was in bad shape. And that was it.

I should have been relieved that she was letting me off the hook that easily, but I couldn't get my brain to shut off. Thera. Eli. Riverwoods. Everyone lying. The hurt look on Thera's face and the resolute line of her mouth when I'd walked out.

A few minutes later, as Mom turned into our neighborhood, with the houses all lit up and welcoming in the dim light of early evening, I couldn't keep from asking the question.

"Is the city trying to take Psychic Mary's house to give to us? The church, I mean."

My mother frowned. "That's not exactly right. I think the city wants to claim it and tear it down to use the land for public improvements."

"Like expanding the road or parking," I said, recalling what Thera had said. Leah's dad and the rest of the council must have been giddy with their victory over the devil worshippers. But what about my dad? Was he on board with this plan?

"That's one possibility," she said. "Where did you hear about all of this?"

"Someone from school." Technically, Thera was someone from school, even if she hadn't told me about it *at* school. "So it is happening."

If my mom knew about it, my dad obviously did too. That made me feel a little queasy. Something about the whole "taking someone's house by force" thing seemed wrong. And yet, what did I know about it? These were my parents; I had a hard time imagining they'd be okay with something shady. My dad had a severe allergy to that, generally speaking, if only because someone might find out about it and he'd lose face.

"It's been discussed," my mom allowed. "I don't know where they are in the process. The congregation hasn't been informed yet, as far as I know. Why are you even thinking about this?"

I ignored her question, having no truthful answer to give, but hesitated before asking mine. "Was Eli . . . Did Eli know about it?"

As always, she flinched slightly when I mentioned his name, as if the letters themselves had sharp edges when arranged in that particular order. "I don't know. I suppose he probably did."

My gut felt hollowed out. I didn't know what to believe about anything or anyone anymore.

"What is this all about?" my mom asked. "Is this about that girl? Thera, you said her name was?" Her hands tightened on the wheel. "Jacob, if you're thinking about going over there again—"

"Never mind. It doesn't matter. Some of Eli's debate team friends were talking at school. I was just curious."

She opened her mouth but closed it again without saying anything as she pulled into the driveway.

Once we were inside, I headed immediately for the stairs to go to my room.

"Dad's at the hospital tonight, sitting with Mr. Thompson, so we're on our own for dinner," Mom said, in a forced cheery tone. "What would you guys like?"

I froze on the third step.

"Daddy's not coming home?" Sarah asked in a small voice.

"Mr. Thompson is being called home to the—" My mom stopped herself.

To the Lord. That's how that sentence would normally go, but with Sarah struggling with the literal and metaphorical as it related to God, Mom was being careful.

"Mr. Thompson is very sick, and Daddy is sitting and praying with him," Mom said instead. "That's Daddy's job, remember?"

My dad often went to the hospitals and nursing homes to sit with sick and dying parishioners or their family members, but he almost always made it home for dinner. Mom would just shift the time to accommodate when he could fit us in. Why not tonight?

"Daddy may end up having to spend the night at the hospital," Mom added in a carefully neutral tone. "He doesn't know for sure yet."

Oh, shit. I turned on the stairs to be able to see my mom in the kitchen. "Dad's not coming home at all?" I asked, incredulous. That had never happened.

"Is Daddy okay?" Sarah asked, her gaze bouncing between us and her eyes welling up.

Mom glared at me. "Sweetie, he's fine. He's just working. Remember what Dr. Monroe said today? Just because you can't see someone doesn't mean something bad has happened to them. Daddy said he'll call you tonight on my phone. You'll be able to use the video chat."

Sarah perked up immediately, tears seemingly forgotten. "Really?"

"Mom—" I began.

"Not now, Jacob," she said almost under her breath. "Sarah, I think you've got a *My Little Pony* episode saved on the DVR. Maybe Jace will watch it with you while I figure out dinner?" She beamed a "you'd better, if you know what's good for you" look at me.

"But I need to change and . . ." *Be alone for a while. Try to understand what happened today.*

Sarah, in the meantime, had begun bouncing from foot to foot, her pink coat making a swishing sound with her eager movements. "Yes, Jace, let's watch! Come on!"

She looked so excited and so not the worried shadow of herself she'd been. How could I say no and crush that?

I was allowed a brief reprieve to change my clothes— which was good because my shirt was a bloody mess—but that was all.

It wasn't until after two episodes and dinner, when Sarah and my mom were finally settled on the couch together, that I could escape upstairs for good.

At the top of the steps, though, instead of heading toward my room, I turned toward Eli's.

Curiosity mixed with doubt flickered in me. If Thera was right, if Eli had been helping her, there would probably be proof of it somewhere in his room.

And I needed to know. Not just whether Thera was telling the truth, but whether Eli was who I thought he'd been.

I could hear the quiet murmur of the TV and the dull roar of laughter from a studio audience. I hoped that would keep Mom and Sarah occupied for a while. If they came upstairs and caught me, I'd have to lie about what I was doing, and I didn't want to have to do that, not with this.

I paused at Eli's door. Stickers from a Relient K concert

and the leadership conference he'd attended last summer were taped to the white panels, where they could be easily removed without damage, per my dad's rules. The edges of the stickers, where he hadn't secured them, moved with my breath. Going inside felt like crossing a threshold in more than the physical sense.

I twisted the handle and eased the door open.

A puff of stale air greeted me, along with a solid darkness inside, which was somehow unnerving. I could see nothing of the room, other than a foot or two of uninteresting beige carpeting caught by the hallway light.

I made myself move forward and fumbled for the light switch. The lamp on his bedside table flared to life.

Everything in here was exactly as I remembered, but with that faint air of disuse. Eli's bed was made, but in a hasty and rumpled way that suggested he'd done it himself before leaving that last day. His laptop sat on the desk, squared off with the edge of it, the cool green "charged" light glowing from the side. The complete Harry Potter series, along with Eli's Patrick Rothfuss and Robert Jordan novels, were on the shelves of his bookcase, beneath the row of debate team trophies and medals, and his textbooks were stacked on the floor by his desk, with the color-coordinated folders and notebooks interspersed. By subject, no doubt.

The punishing ache of missing him struck suddenly and so hard, it felt like it would never let up.

I missed my brother, my twin. And he wasn't coming back. I would never see him again. Sometimes that idea seemed so impossible.

I stepped farther into the room and closed the door quietly behind me. A name badge ("Elijah Palmer, River-woods Bible Church") on a thin lanyard, hanging on the back of the door, clacked softly against the white faux wood. It was a room full of all the pieces that made up my brother, but they were not Eli, just souvenirs that pointed to a place that no longer existed.

A clear plastic dry-cleaning bag rested in the center of his bed. In it, a piece of clothing was folded neatly, the plastic pulled tightly against the surface.

The words on the front had been almost obliterated by a deep brown stain and a smooth slash up the center, the edges of fabric curling away from the cut, but I recognized them.

BIG TALK, BIG WALK.

My mom had brought Eli's debate team sweatshirt back to him.

Stupidly, even though it was my blood all over the front of it and not Eli's, I half wanted to tear into the plastic covering to touch the sweatshirt, as if it might transport me to him or that last night so that I could save him.

I sank onto the edge of the bed and listened to the springs groan, a familiar sound from when we'd shared a room a long time ago or when I would wake up in the middle of the night and hear him shifting on his bed across the hall.

Forcing my attention back to his room, I tried to figure out where to start. I didn't know what I was looking for, only that it was probably hidden.

His laptop seemed as good a place as any to begin.

After flipping the screen up, I hit the power button, and as I waited, I sat in his chair and searched his desk drawers.

They contained absolutely nothing unexpected. A few pictures of Leah and him. Some stray scripture/prayer cards that someone had given him. In the deeper drawers, he'd meticulously filed old papers, speeches, and assorted "important" documents.

I flipped through them quickly, but the contents in each file seemed to match the printed label on the tab. His "important" documents were mostly college brochures with his notes on applying for financial aid as well as what appeared to be a running list of his accomplishments.

None of that surprised me.

Once Eli's laptop was up and humming, I went straight to his browser history.

But his searches were all mundane, boring. Along with obvious debate topics (right to die, the ethics of corporate donations to political campaigns, abortion), he'd been researching colleges, competing debate teams, local restaurants, movie times, and various scripture and theology sites.

The only semi-strange thing was a bunch of searches on something called sunshine laws, which seemed to be about access to local government meetings and freedom of information.

That could have been about Thera's house. But it also might have been research for a debate or a paper. With Eli, it was hard to know.

It wasn't enough.

I opened his email to be sure, but at a quick glance, his sent box contained nothing controversial. Homework, student council agendas, emails to Leah.

A quick search of his files didn't show anything out of the ordinary, but Eli was so detailed—every folder had subfolders—that it would take me years to get through everything. When I ran a search for documents modified the week before the accident, though, nothing came up.

I sighed and swiveled in his chair to stare out at his room. I didn't really know what I was looking for, and there were too many possible places to check, assuming there was something to find at all.

The battered Bible on his nightstand, shining in the light from the lamp, caught my eye. It was the same as the one I'd received in third grade, a gold cover covering tissue-paper-thin pages.

If Eli was keeping a secret, odds were he felt conflicted about it. And if it was important, he might want it near him, like the Bible.

I walked to the nightstand and scooped up his Bible. It fell open easily in my hands, multiple verses underlined on every page I could see, with Eli's neat handwriting in the margins. In Mark, after Jesus heals the blind man who initially describes people as walking trees: "Why trees? Ref to tree of knowledge or life?" In Luke, near the story about the woman with the bleeding illness: "Faith comes first. Then healing. Same pattern."

He'd stuck a photo of Leah in the pages, to keep it safe or maybe as a bookmark. I could see the top of her head and her eyes. When I flipped to that page— Matthew 10, with verse 37 highlighted: "Whoever loves father or mother more than me is not worthy of me; and whoever loves son or daughter more is not worthy of me"—the rest of her face was revealed, softer and happier than I'd ever seen it. Eli had obviously been the one to take the photo.

The lump in my throat grew. I'd destroyed that, too. Not only him, but the two of them.

It was so strange to think of him lying here at night, right here, looking at Leah's picture and reading verses, only a few months ago. It felt like there should be a way to reach back, like that segment of time should still be close enough to touch, to warn him not to answer my call.

He'd been sitting right here on the edge of the bed when I came to bug him about taking the car. If I'd just stayed in . . .

Something caught at my memory, like a lurch in the feed, and I replayed the moment in my mind, the final time we'd both been home.

Eli, sitting on the edge of his bed, shoving the night-stand drawer shut, but it was the guilty look on his face that captured my attention both then and now. I'd let it go then, in my pursuit of getting the Jeep.

But now . . .

Setting his Bible aside, I pulled out the bedside table drawer hurriedly. A ChapStick rolled to the front, clacking loudly against the faux wood panel. Beyond that, there wasn't much in here—a box of tissues, a half-empty bottle of lotion, an outdated bottle of nasal spray, and a bunch more pictures of him with Leah.

A weird mix of disappointment and relief surged through me. I'd thought for sure I was onto something.

I went to shove the drawer back in, but it caught in the frame, forcing the drawer to the side at an angle.

I pulled the drawer back out and tried again, pushing harder. Only this time, the resistance was accompanied by the thin protest of tearing paper.

After removing the drawer from the nightstand, I

lifted it up, ducking my head to see beneath it. A manila folder was duct-taped to the bottom of the drawer.

Just like in that ridiculous Jason Bourne rip-off movie we'd seen a couple of years ago, one that he'd hated because he said it underestimated the audience's intelligence.

The fact that he'd imitated it anyway made me want to laugh, even as my vision went blurry with tears.

I made myself draw a deep breath and turn my attention to the folder. The front of it was now ripped, thanks to my efforts to jam the drawer into place, and I could see the top of a few printed pages as well as a swath of Eli's precise handwriting on one sheet. Thera's last name, Catoulus, jumped out at me in several places.

I tipped the drawer on its side on the bed, sending half the contents tumbling out onto the comforter, and yanked at the folder. The tape gave reluctantly at first, and then with a loud ripping noise.

I paused, listening for footsteps approaching, but heard nothing.

Pushing the drawer out of the way, I sat on the edge of the bed and opened the folder.

The first page was simply a printout, similar to the one I'd seen with Thera in the library, with the term "eminent domain" and the basic definition and process. Boring, nothing useful there.

I flipped a few more pages and found more print-outs, more research. This time, it was on that sunshine law stuff, and it was mostly from the McHenry Hills city website. One page had several lines highlighted: "shall be considered applicable if three city council members (a quorum) are present and the meeting *must* be open to the public, or said members are in violation. Violations must be reported to the Illinois Office of the Attorney General within sixty days."

After that, I found copies of the letters sent to Thera and Mary from Riverwoods and then the city. The first offer from Riverwoods had been $80,000, and the last one from the city, in December, had been $45,000. That last letter also included the information that if they chose not to accept the offer, McHenry Hills would move forward with a vote to take their property.

What was this? There was no bombshell in here any-where. It was a bunch of research and stuff Thera already had or knew. The only sign that it might be something significant, as far as I could tell, was that Eli had hidden it.

Confused, I turned to the back, where I'd glimpsed Eli's handwriting.

The last page in the folder was a single sheet of note-book paper covered on the front and back with Eli's notes in neat paragraphs, labeled by date, starting in October of last year.

The beginning was a few lines that indicated that he'd heard Mr. Hauer, Mr. McKinney, and Mr. Greeley, all Riverwoods members and, apparently, council members for the city, discussing expansion plans and the need for land on multiple occasions while he, Eli, was at church, working. He even listed other witnesses to the conversations: Delores and Carol.

As I continued reading, noting the formality of his language, pieces began to fall into place. Eli was building a case. I'd seen him do this hundreds of times before, usually with index cards, when he was creating an argument for debate team.

In November, according to his notes, he'd asked Mr. Hauer about the city's offer to the Catouluses. That must have been when Thera and her mom first received the letter; she said Eli was there when they got it. And, of course, Eli had plenty of opportunity to talk to Hauer about it, given that he was Leah's dad and Eli had been over there almost every night.

"I was told that everything was well in hand and that, as he'd reassured my father, they would be 'killing two birds with one stone,' eliminating 'a stain on the community,' and building a better future for Riverwoods."

That didn't sound good. Wasn't the government supposed to be impartial or whatever?

It clicked then. That was exactly it. Mr. Hauer and the

others weren't impartial, and that was the point of all of this. Eli had started investigating what was happening to Thera, seeing it as an injustice, and discovered that there was some level of corruption in the process.

Corruption, I realized belatedly, that included my dad.

Was that why Eli had backed off and told Thera he couldn't go through with it? And why he hadn't told me about it?

Now I couldn't decide which was less Eli-like: that he'd taken on a fight that put him in direct opposition to River-woods, or that he'd walked away before finishing it. This was exactly the kind of ethics debate he loved arguing. Eli liked nothing more than to set up camp on the moral high ground.

I flipped the page over to continue reading. In December, Eli had written that he'd "witnessed the meeting of the same Riverwoods members and city council officials at the Hauer house in a discussion about the Catoulus prop-erty, while visiting ~~my girlfriend,~~ Leah Hauer."

Was he trying to make it sound as professional as pos-sible, or was he actually worried about his relationship with Leah? From the sounds of all of this, he was aim-ing to bring trouble of some kind down on Mr. Hauer and the others, so maybe it wasn't that big a leap that he would have been concerned about his future with Leah once it all came out.

The next line, the second-to-last entry, was simply a note with the date in December, indicating that the Catouluses had received a final offer from the McHenry Hills City Council. About three days after Mr. Hauer was holding that private meeting in his house.

He'd rigged it. After Thera and Mary turned down Riverwoods' offer, Mr. Hauer had pushed it through the city council to take their land.

I sat back, springs in the mattress creaking beneath me. There was no way Eli could ignore that—not even with his love for Riverwoods and Leah.

Except he had. Because the process was still going on.

The final paragraph was written in a different color pen—blue rather than black—and his writing seemed slanted and hurried. It was on December 27, a week before he died, and those last lines were very likely the last piece of writing Eli had done.

"While visiting the Hauer house, I contrived to be alone with Mr. Hauer momentarily. I intended to hand over the information I'd collected to Thera Catoulus for her to pass along to a lawyer. It seemed only fair to give Mr. Hauer a chance to address the facts and change his course of action before it was too late."

Eli. I shook my head.

I could have told Eli that Mr. Hauer wouldn't go for it. I didn't know the guy nearly as well as Eli did, but obviously, Leah's dad had way too much invested in doing what he considered "right." But Eli wasn't one to let things go, especially not something like this.

"Mr. Hauer was displeased to hear the details I'd assembled as well as my intention for them. He explained how it was all for the good of the church and the community. 'Sometimes you have to bend a few rules to make the world a better place. You know that, son.'"

My palms began to sweat. I could see the train wreck coming, Eli and Mr. Hauer heading straight for each other at full speed on the same track.

"Mr. Hauer proceeded to discuss the outcome of my potential action. 'Think of the damage to your legacy. Your family has been essential to Riverwoods from the beginning. But then again, I guess nothing lasts forever. And as the church council president, sometimes I'm asked to make difficult decisions.' Though he did not directly say, I believe this veiled threat was meant to indicate that he would seek to remove my father from his position as head pastor at Riverwoods."

Holy shit.

"As if fearing that would not be enough, he then threatened more personal consequences. 'If all goes as planned, it's only a few more years before you're back here to minister in this community that your father and grandfather have worked so hard to build. It would be a shame if that didn't work out. I know Leah would be disappointed.'"

Riverwoods. His future. Leah. Everything Eli cared about. Hauer knew him well enough to read every page in his book.

Fury on Eli's behalf crashed through me, making my hands clench around the edges of the folder. Mr. Hauer had no right to threaten him like that. If I'd been there, the conversation would have gone differently. I didn't have nearly as much to lose in telling Mr. Hauer to shove it.

The last line was almost illegible and tilted halfway down to the blank line below it: "This is wrong. But I have no proof, other than my testimony of what I've witnessed."

To anyone else, it might have looked like a simple statement of fact, a summing up of the previous entries.

But to me, despair and frustration screamed from every loop and slash of his handwriting in that sentence. It was an acknowledgment of Mr. Hauer's position and power, and Eli's lack of it. Not to mention the potential consequences if Eli kept going.

Then, six days after this conversation, according to Thera, Eli had come over to her house and told her that he couldn't help her.

He'd given in and walked away, abandoning Thera and her mother, people who needed help.

I sat back, my head spinning. My brother, the "good twin," had faltered. That conversation in the Jeep that last night wasn't about Thera and her house, not specifically. It was about Eli, about him trying to justify the decision he'd made.

In our family, I was always the selfish one, the short-sighted one, the superficial one.

But apparently, I wasn't the only flawed one. Eli had messed up. He'd gone against everything he believed was right because he was afraid. I didn't know how to reconcile that information with the brother I knew.

But if I didn't know who Eli was, who was I, really? Then and now? We were supposed to be opposites, two halves of a whole. But if I was wrong about him, it was like losing track of the ball in the sun. I was blind and lost, without a point of reference.

What shook me more than anything, though, was that he'd never said anything to me about any of this, other than that one cryptic conversation on that last night.

Why not? Did he think I would judge him, like Kylie had said at lunch today? That I wouldn't have listened or tried to help?

Maybe . . . Maybe I wouldn't have. Not back then.

But I was changing, growing without him here. Did I want that? Did I have a choice?

I had to get out of here. I couldn't handle this right now.

I slapped the folder shut and reattached it to the bottom of the drawer, using the floppy and sagging pieces of tape. Then I stood and put everything back in the drawer as quietly as I could and replaced it in the nightstand.

Before stepping back, I pushed at Eli's comforter, trying to straighten out the dent from where I'd sat on it. It needed to look like I'd never been here.

I needed to never have been here.

CHAPTER TWENTY-FOUR

I WAS IN A familiar hallway, doors lining both sides in both directions as far as I could see. I could hear the rush of wind from somewhere and the rustling of the papers at my feet. The pages, which were blank, covered the dark red carpet in thick patches, like fallen leaves in perfect white rectangles.

In front of me, the closest door stood open. I didn't remember it opening, but I also didn't remember finding this particular door among the many. It was just here, and so was I.

And when I looked through the doorway, my twin was waiting in the otherwise empty space. He grinned at me and held a hand up in greeting. He was wearing his stupid church camp T-shirt beneath his open button-down, like when I'd last seen him.

"Eli, hey," I said in relief, a sense of well-being flooding through me. He would fix everything. Life would go back to normal now. I didn't have to figure anything out.

I started toward him, but his eyes widened in alarm and he pointed down at the threshold between us. His mouth moved rapidly, but I couldn't hear him.

Not like before, when I could hear him but couldn't find him.

Before.

Wait. Had I been here before? When?

I frowned, trying to remember. I realized I didn't even know for sure where I was.

Eli raked his hand through his hair in frustration, drawing my attention back to him. He took a deep breath then, as if working for patience, and I could see his chest rise and fall with it.

You. He mouthed the word carefully, pointing to me and then to the papers on the ground, giving me a significant look.

"You want these?" I asked, bending to scoop up a handful and hold them out to him. It was an easy movement, pain-free and smooth in a way that I'd not experienced in months.

I stared down at the pages in my left hand. My elbow was fully extended, and it didn't hurt. There were no tremors or shooting pains. And when I turned my arm to see the underside, the surgery scars were gone.

It was like the accident had never happened.

The accident. I'd been hurt and Eli . . . Eli had been killed.

Reality came rushing into this space that seemed to exist outside of it, or alongside.

"What . . . ," I began, not sure how to ask. "How are you here?"

He looked at me, his expression sad but knowing, like he was waiting for me to catch up.

And then I did.

"You're dead. This isn't real," I whispered.

After a pause, he gave a single bob of his head in acknowledgment.

My eyes burned with tears, and my lower lip started to tremble. I covered my face with my good arm. "What are you doing here? What is this?" I choked out. It was bad enough that I had to live my awake-life without him—now I was being tortured in dreams too?

A noise came from in front of me, like the odd sound a handsaw makes when you bend the blade. My grandpa used to do it to make us laugh.

I lowered my arm. Eli was still there, his fists pressed against an invisible barrier in the doorway. But he was scowling at me now, the way he used to when I took too much time in the bathroom or when I turned off the Jeep and left the fan on high.

Eli shook his head and pointed at the papers on the ground and in my hand.

I stared at the pages and then back at him, in confusion. "What do you want me to do with these? They're all blank."

He gave me a strange look.

I held up the fistful I'd gathered a moment ago to show him. But as I watched, a thick black scrawl appeared on the pages, filling every inch of the blank space. Only, I couldn't read any of it. The words were jumbled and out of order, or weren't words at all—at least, not in a language I recognized.

When I tried to read one of the pages anyway, the squiggles and letters shifted and reordered themselves, making it impossible.

Panic flooded my chest, that tight, squeezing sensation that made it feel like all the air was being pushed out of my lungs. I had to be able to read these pages.

"Eli, how am I supposed to . . ." I glanced up and found him several feet farther back from the doorway than he was a moment ago.

And he was slowly walking—no, being pulled backward—away from the door. Away from me.

"No!" I lunged at the door, only to be pushed back by an unseen force.

"Wait! You have to stay," I called after him, desperate.

"You can't leave me here with these. I don't know what to do!"

Growing more distant by the second, he smiled and waved at me, as if he couldn't hear or understand what I was saying. Or he didn't care anymore.

"No, Eli, wait!" I shouted after him. "Wait, please. Eli, you have to tell me—"

I woke up abruptly, heart pounding, mouth dry, my eyes gritty with sleep and filled with unshed tears.

It took me a second to process where and when I was. In my room, Friday, no, Saturday morning.

I turned my head on the pillow to see my alarm clock. 8:47 a.m.

Closing my eyes again, I tried to slow my breathing and my heart rate.

I shouldn't have taken that second pain pill before bed last night, no matter how much I was hurting. That, in combination with what I'd found in Eli's room, had obviously—

No. I wasn't going there.

I didn't know what to do about that folder, couldn't even think about it. It made me feel like my skin didn't fit quite right when I did.

But lying there, trying not to think about it, or anything else, I remembered what Thera's mother had said yesterday. *He wants you to finish what he started.*

I pushed myself out of bed and scavenged a pair of basketball shorts from the floor to pull on over my boxers.

When I opened the door to my room, the smell of bacon and coffee floated up, making my stomach growl. I'd retreated to my room early last night, exhausted from the day and the fight and also not sure I could face my mom and my sister without them noticing something was wrong.

But this morning, the tempting scent of food combined with the demands of an empty stomach forced me to try. I made my way down the steps, listening to the clank of pans and the sizzle of food in the kitchen.

I expected the low murmur of voices, my mom talking to my dad or the two of them talking to Sarah.

Instead, I found Sarah curled on a stool at the island, picking at her eggs and looking half asleep.

"Oh, good, you're up." My mom turned away from the stove and grabbed a plate from the island. "I was just going to try to wake you." She squinted at me. "I think the swelling in your nose is down, but your eye is certainly more colorful."

I made a face. "Thanks." I took a seat on the other stool, next to Sarah.

Mom picked up a spatula and began loading my plate with scrambled eggs.

"Where's Dad?" My voice came out sounding rusty from disuse.

Her hands stilled. "He came home for a few minutes this morning to shower, and now he's at church, writing and rehearsing his sermon," she said.

Uh-oh.

She resumed filling my plate, plucking bacon out of a glass dish on the stove top.

"When's he coming home?" I asked, pushing back against the scrabbling claws of unease. I didn't particularly want him home yelling at me. But neither did I want to lose another piece of my already fractured and disintegrating family. We were like shards of a shattered mirror, hanging in the frame by the form we used to have but slowly falling out, one by one. And the longer my dad was gone, the more it would start to feel like a real absence, something that couldn't be glossed over or forgotten.

"I want to see Daddy," Sarah added. "For real, not on the phone."

My mom turned to hand me the plate. "We'll see, sweetie," she said to Sarah. "It depends on Daddy's schedule. You know how busy it is during Lent."

"But I want to—" Sarah began, working herself up to a full whine, only to be interrupted by the doorbell.

For a moment, the three of us just looked at each other in surprise. Who would be coming over without warning this early on a Saturday?

"Maybe Daddy forgot his keys," Sarah ventured.

Mom winced. "I'll get it. It's probably Lolly from down the street. I ordered some cookie dough for a fund-raiser," she said. "You stay and eat."

"Sares, do you have an extra fork over there?" I asked.

"I have my fork," Sarah said, licking the utensil in question. "But I'm done. You can have it." She held it out to me.

I made a face. "No, thanks."

I slid off my stool and headed for the silverware drawer.

"Jace."

Turning, I found my mom at the threshold of the hallway and the kitchen with an odd expression on her face. "Someone's here to see you."

"Who?" Immediately my mind conjured the last visitor I'd had. "If it's Leah, I can't—"

"It's not Leah," she said. "You should go." Her tone seemed strained, and yet she was encouraging me to go to the door.

"Okay," I said slowly, turning away from the drawer. Her weirdness was kind of freaking me out.

But when I got to the hallway and the partially open front door, I saw the reason for it.

Thera was on my front porch. She was rocking back and forth, as if on starter blocks for a race and waiting for the gun. Her dark hair was pulled back into a messy ponytail, and the hood on her sweatshirt beneath her battered leather coat was halfway up, as if she'd been reluctant to pull it down to begin with. She was beautiful, as always, and if the color in her cheeks was any indication, she was either really cold or really angry. Possibly both.

"Hey," I said, stunned. I pulled the door open the rest of the way, but reflexively looked over my shoulder for one or more of my parents, who under normal circumstances—maybe in a life that was no longer mine—would be hovering barely out of sight. "What are you doing—"

"Your mom asked if I wanted to come in. I said no," Thera said, lifting her chin. "I just have two things to say to you."

I edged out, shivering in the cold—shorts and a T-shirt were no match for March—and pulled the door mostly shut behind me for privacy. "Thera—"

"First. You left this in my car." She handed over my backpack, loaded down with all Mrs. Rafferty's yearbook examples.

I took it, the weight of it pulling me forward. "Thanks," I said. I'd forgotten all about it until now.

"Eli deserves a memorial page, and you don't have the right to screw that up because you want to avoid me," she said.

I flinched. "I wasn't going to—"

"Second. You don't have to believe me about Eli." She let out a soft breath that wreathed her face in white. "I honestly think he would have changed his mind and come through for us in the end."

No, he wouldn't have. My guilt and confusion over what I'd found roared back at full force.

"But that doesn't matter now. What does is what you said to me." She swiped at her watering eyes angrily with a shaking hand. "I didn't kiss you or let you touch me to convince you of something. If you really believe I did, then you're not who I thought you were. You're no better than Doug and Aaron and those other baseball assholes who think it's my fault what happened last year."

Tears left bright shiny tracks on her red cheeks, despite her efforts to wipe them away, and the sight of them tore at me.

"Thera." I reached out for her. "I am so sorry."

But she spun away from me. "I'm done now," she said over her shoulder as she pulled her hood up.

Thera strode down the two brick steps to our sidewalk, heading for her battered car parked in the street. The one and only person who'd made my life better, who'd been willing to accept me for who I was now, damaged, broken and lost, was walking away, for good. She was innocent in all of this mess, too, the one who'd be hurt the most by other people making decisions she couldn't control.

Was I really going to let her go because I was confused, because not everything was exactly like I thought it was or should be? That seemed wrong. Like the action of a person I didn't want to be. Or didn't want to be anymore.

Do something. The urgency in me built to a breaking point.

"You were right," I called after her, the words slightly too loud in my desire to make sure she heard me. They seemed to echo off the frozen landscape, hard and harsh; but like a breath of that cold bracing air, saying the words aloud brought along a sweeping sensation of being cleansed.

Thera slowed, then stopped, turning to face me. "What?"

"I know you were telling the truth. About everything," I admitted, the confession coming easier now that I'd started.

She eyed me with suspicion, as if expecting a sudden reversal or a trick.

"I'm sorry," I said again, pleading. "I was so caught up in trying to figure out what I believed, I lost track of who to believe."

She shook her head, but she didn't walk away. Which was more than I deserved.

Please let this be the right thing to do. I offered up the silent prayer to God, my brother, anyone who might be listening; then I moved back, making room in the doorway.

"You should come in," I said.

CHAPTER TWENTY-FIVE

THERA STEPPED INTO OUR house with the wariness of someone expecting an attack from all sides.

"Come on." I shut the door and waved her forward, leading the way to the kitchen.

"Are you sure this is a good idea?" she asked.

"It'll be fine," I said, though I wasn't absolutely sure about that. But we definitely had better odds with only my mom and Sarah home.

My mom, having returned to her position behind the island, went still when she saw Thera behind me.

"Mom, this is Thera Catoulus. She's been helping me with . . . stuff. She brought my backpack back to me. I forgot it after my fall yesterday."

Mom nodded uncertainly, the spatula in her hands,

like she was holding the situation at bay with the flat plastic end as a shield.

"Thera, this is my mom, Carrie Palmer."

Thera rallied faster, pausing only slightly before stepping forward and offering her hand to my mom over the expanse of the island counter. "Nice to meet you," she said.

My mom transferred her spatula to one hand and shook Thera's with the other. "You too," she said.

"And this is my sister, Sarah," I said.

Sarah, who'd been staring at Thera this whole time, cocked her bed-tangled head to one side. "Do you like the boys better at St. Luke's? Jace's old girlfriend does."

"Sarah!" my mom scolded.

I groaned.

"Uh, actually, I don't know any. I don't think," Thera said, stuffing her hands into her jacket pockets.

Sarah nodded, seemingly satisfied with that answer. "Okay."

"Thera, can I make you something to eat? We were just sitting down to breakfast," my mom said hesitantly.

"No, I'm fine, thank you, Mrs. Palmer," Thera said, shooting me a look that said "get to it."

"Actually, I have something I wanted to show Thera upstairs real quick." I headed that way, nudging Thera as I passed so she'd come along.

"But your eggs will be cold," my mom said with a warning frown. *Visitors aren't allowed upstairs.*

"It won't take long. I'll be back in a few minutes." I
wasn't asking for permission.

I started up the stairs, with Thera a step behind me.

"Keep your door open, Jacob," my mom called when
we were about halfway up.

My face went hot, and Thera inhaled sharply.

"She didn't mean anything by it. It's just the rules," I
murmured to her.

"Whatever."

At the top of the staircase, I turned and opened the
door to Eli's room. Then I moved back to allow Thera in
and closed the door after her.

Thera raised her eyebrows.

"*My* door is open," I pointed out. "And I really do have
something to show you."

"Eli's room?" she asked quietly, hovering near the
entrance.

"Yeah."

She surveyed the room, taking it all in. Her breath
caught when she noticed the sweatshirt in the plastic bag
on the bed.

"I was wearing it the night of the accident, borrowed it
from him when Kylie spilled beer on me," I said. "I think
my mom brought it back for him."

Thera bit her lip.

She stepped in deeper to look at his bookcase, and I moved to the nightstand. We wouldn't have a whole lot of time up here before my mom came to check on us, I was sure.

"I knew he was a fantasy geek," she said with fondness, running fingers lightly along the spines of his books. "We used to argue about that. Science fiction versus fantasy."

"There's a difference?" I asked, tugging the drawer out with a grunt of effort.

She didn't answer. "What are you doing?" she asked, moving to my side as I set the drawer on the bed.

I tipped the drawer over, revealing the folder taped to the bottom of it.

She gasped. "You found it."

"I'm sorry I didn't believe you. But I'm not sure it's . . ." I paused. "I just thought you should see it." Though I wasn't exactly sure how she'd react. She might be angry, and she deserved to be.

After pulling the folder free, I handed it to her.

She hesitated for a second, then took it and flipped it open carefully.

I stepped back, keeping an ear out for the sound of my mom coming up the stairs. We'd have to have a hell of an excuse if she caught us in here. I strained to hear anything from the kitchen below, but my mom and my sister were being too quiet.

I watched Thera's expression as she moved through the pages, her forehead wrinkling with concentration or confusion or both.

And when she reached the last page, Eli's handwritten notes, I held my breath.

Thera would be well within her rights to start yelling. At me, at Eli, at everyone involved.

Thera's shoulders tensed, and I braced myself, as she turned the page over.

A few minutes later, she sagged into herself. "He should have told me," she said.

I was trying to understand that too. Thinking like Eli would have, I could only come up with one answer. "I think he might have been embarrassed. People always see us . . . saw us . . . as in relation to the other. If I was the bad one, then he had to be the good one. But I think this was maybe making him question . . . everything." Actually, there was no maybe about it. He'd said as much in the car to me that night; I just hadn't known what he was talking about.

She closed the folder and smoothed the front, like a gesture of good-bye, and then held it out to me. Her eyes were damp with tears.

"You're not angry?" I asked in disbelief, taking the folder.

"Angry that someone threatened him? Yes. That he was scared and backed off? No."

"Why not?"

"He was my friend. He was trying to help me, which is more than anyone else did," she said. "I appreciate that, more than he'll ever know. But it was self-preservation. I get that, probably better than anyone. Expecting someone to do the right thing at a cost to themselves . . ." She shook her head.

But they should. They were supposed to, weren't they? Wasn't that exactly what Eli had been struggling with?

"Plus, I'm not sure it would have worked even if he had gone through it," Thera said. "It would have been his word against theirs."

And Eli, no matter how smart and serious he was, would have been seen as just a kid, not worth taking seriously. And that was only if anyone bothered to look into the situation. So it would have been exactly as he'd feared—giving up everything and changing nothing.

"But thank you for showing me." She smiled, wiping under her eyes. "It's nice to know I was right about him. That he really was trying."

I ran my hand through my hair in frustration. "It's not right," I said. "They shouldn't be able to do this." The contents of the folder had shifted, and the Riverwoods letterhead logo, the Dove of Peace, now poked out at the top, like a taunt. It killed me how closely my family was involved in this mess.

"It'll be okay," Thera said, sounding tired. "I'll probably get to finish the year here. Then I'll have to figure it out. I can maybe find us an apartment somewhere nearby, and Mom does have some phone and web clients, so the business won't close completely. I'll have to see what I can do to make some extra money."

She was going to end up quitting school; I could see it coming right at her, the choice between building a future and maintaining her present. She'd choose the present for her mother. She would have to. And that was just *wrong*.

"There has to be something else." I wished, suddenly, violently, for the days when I went to my parents with all of my problems—a skinned knee, the monster in the back of the closet, the need for a drink of water in the middle of the night—and every problem seemed easily solvable as soon as they were involved. But in this case, I couldn't be sure that my dad wasn't part of the problem. Eli had clearly thought that was a possibility, which was why he hadn't gone to my dad with any of it. At least, that's what I assumed. Or maybe the embarrassment that kept him from telling Thera also kept him from sharing what was going on with my dad. Either way, I doubted my dad would be the most receptive audience now. I didn't want him to be the bad guy, but the truth was, he had too much at stake with Mr. Hauer and the expansion.

Thera lifted her shoulders in a helpless shrug.

"The lawyer we talked to said that the hearing might work in our favor. We can't afford to fight this in court. But he has some media contacts, and if we hire him, he'll use them to try to draw enough public attention to shame the city into a higher offer, something closer to what Riverwoods offered originally." She rolled her eyes. "But that might be his hope for a bigger piece of the settlement talking. I've been doing some research online, trying to figure out the numbers. By the time we're done with taxes and fees, I'm not sure what'll be left." She sounded a decade older than she should have, a full-on adult.

Public attention. Shame. Riverwoods. The words were hot pokers, jabbing individually into my brain. I could practically feel the sear of the metal. And they were followed by the phrase that had hung over my head every time we left the house for as long as I could remember: *Someone is always watching and we have an obligation to be good examples.*

Bullshit. It was all bullshit. And someone needed to do something about it. Or at least *try.*

A brief scene from my dream last night resurfaced—Eli pointing at me, mouthing the word "you."

The image raised goose bumps on my arms, and the first vague outlines of an idea began to form in my head. It scared the hell out of me, but at the same time, it felt right, the first thing to feel that way in a long time.

"Jacob?" My mom called from downstairs, her voice muffled and faint.

I crept to Eli's door and cracked it open. "Be right there," I shouted.

"Are you all right?" Thera asked with a frown. "You had this really weird look on your face."

"It's fine," I said. "I'm fine." I took a deep breath. "I need to get dressed, but can you give me a ride some-where?"

CHAPTER TWENTY-SIX

WHEN I WALKED IN, the new building was quiet but for the distant hum of the furnace, and most of the lights were off. Delores and Carol weren't here yet, and I didn't hear any typing noises from the office.

The main entrance had been unlocked, though, and my dad's Escalade was in its space, so he was here somewhere.

My gaze drifted from the hallway that led to my dad's office to the shiny wooden double doors of the auditorium in front of me. They were closed. He was probably in there, rehearsing already. He liked to run through his sermon a few times with no one around.

I hadn't been in the auditorium since before the accident. It was where they'd held Eli's funeral service.

I could easily imagine it, the room packed to the gills

with people and that lonely casket on the center stage. My family—minus me—clustered around it.

The rush of emptiness, of missing Eli, swelled again, and for one quick second, I thought about turning around and walking back out to the lot, where Thera was waiting for me.

Back at my house, I'd told my mom we needed to work on Eli's page for the yearbook at school. She didn't believe me, but with Sarah and Thera there to overhear, she was forced to keep her protests limited and vague. And I'd promised to be back in an hour.

Then once Thera and I were in the car, I told her where I really wanted to go.

"You don't have to do this," she said.

"Yeah, I do," I said with a certainty that was rare these days.

"Do you think it's going to change anything?" she said. "It's too late for that."

"I don't know. It might not. But I feel like I have to try," I said, uncomfortable with that reality.

My whole life, I'd kind of coasted along and never paid much attention to anyone or anything else. I'd avoided situations as soon as they got complicated. It felt easier. And as long as Eli was around to be the kind and conscientious one, I could get away with it. I was just playing my role, being his other half. But now, with him gone, I was seeing things differently. Eli wasn't always the one who got it right. I wasn't always the screwup.

This situation with Thera and her mother and River-woods was wrong. There was no way around that, even for someone as unstudied and uncertain in their beliefs as me. Eli had tried to fix it, but he'd had too much to lose.

I didn't, not anymore. And I was awake now—that was what it felt like. I couldn't go back to sleep.

Plus, my dad should know exactly what Mr. Hauer had done and said to Eli. *No one* was allowed to mess with Eli like that. He might be dead—maybe gone forever—but he was still my brother. My twin.

I'd done my best to explain all of that to Thera. She'd watched me for a second, as if evaluating my sincerity, my motives, or both, and then started the car.

When I pulled at the handle, the auditorium door opened smoothly and silently—no squeaking hinges to shame the latecomers at Riverwoods. The room itself was hushed and dark, the only light coming from the spotlight focused on the lectern at center stage and the metal dove sculpture hanging on the wall behind it.

My dad, his hair rumpled and far from TV ready, stood at the lectern, his glasses balanced on the end of his nose and pages in his hand.

"In this passage from John, the Pharisees are questioning Jesus about his miracle, healing this man on the

Sabbath. They question Jesus in every way possible, including whether the man was actually blind to begin with." He spoke fervently to an invisible crowd of congregants.

I made my way down the nearest aisle. This big open space didn't have the weight and solemnity of the original sanctuary, the one where Eli and I had been baptized. Decorated in dark colors and plush fabrics—all chosen with an eye toward how they would appear on the television broadcast—the auditorium lacked the brightness and life, for lack of better words, that existed in traditional church buildings.

Even still, the silence in here was familiar, a sense of waiting. Not a presence, exactly, but an immediacy and awareness that didn't exist elsewhere. Like a place and a moment in time when you were supposed to pay attention, to be here and not caught up in stats or pitching strategies for next week's game.

But unlike during my last visit to church, the urge to flee did not strike this time. Maybe I'd changed. Or maybe just having a purpose helped. "The man's family and neighbors are too frightened of the Pharisees and possible repercussions to testify otherwise. So what exactly is Jesus telling us here?"

My dad stopped, then mumbled, "Leave a pause." He bent his head down to scrawl a note on the pages in front of him.

"We have a saying, 'Seeing is believing,'" he continued. "But the truth is, we will always encounter doubters, those who are put on our path to test us. Seeing is not the same thing as understanding. The blind man understood and believed, even before Jesus restored his sight. But our doubters, our detractors, will always find reasons to see but not understand."

When I reached the gap between the first row of seats and the stage, my dad caught sight of the motion.

He lifted his hand to block the spotlight. "Jace?" He left the lectern, heading to the edge of the stage, concern creasing his forehead. "What are you doing here? Is everything okay?"

"Everything's fine." I stuffed my hands in my pockets. "I just need to talk to you about something."

"Oh." He frowned at me. "Your face looks worse than your mother said."

So they had at least spoken. That was good. I guess.

"If this is about the *fight* you were in"—he looked at me pointedly, letting me know that my bullshit about a fall wasn't flying with him—"you'll have to wait. I need to finish here and then I have to go back to the hospital. Mr. Thompson's daughter is flying in. After that, I have to call the Underhills back."

Crap. I forgot. Caleb's parents came here sometimes. They were members, even if they weren't regulars.

"I was defending someone else," I said. "Doesn't that matter?"

My dad held up a hand, dismissing my words as he turned back to the lectern. "Your job is to set a good example. How many times have we told you that?"

"Yeah, but, Dad, how far does that go?" I asked. "Am I supposed to let Caleb say and do whatever he wants, no matter who gets hurt?"

He sighed. "You're twisting my words, Jacob, and I don't have time—"

"Or is being a good example only more important when it comes to defending Thera Catoulus? If it was someone else, would it have been okay then?"

He faced me. "I told you to stay away from her," he said, pointing a finger at me.

"I know," I said. "Because you don't want me to mess up the deal."

"Jacob, I've already explained to you why this is important—"

"More important than doing the right thing?" I asked. "Dad, please. I'm trying to understand this, I really am, but—"

"It's a complicated situation, and you only *think* you know everything," he said, looking past me like I didn't exist. Then he stalked back to the lectern and gathered up his pages.

Anger flickered to life in me. I moved to the edge of the stage, laying my hands flat on the floor of it. "Did you know? About Mr. Hauer? What they're doing?"

His hands, busy rearranging pages, stilled, and my heart sank. "Riverwoods made the Catouluses a fair offer and they turned it down. What the city chooses to do of its own accord—"

"Bullshit," I said.

He lurched forward at me, and it took effort for me not to jump back. "You have no idea!" he shouted. "No idea what's at stake!"

"But you're trying to fix something by breaking something else, and that's not right. We're supposed to look out for the people who need help. Isn't that the point of being here, being part of the church? Feed the hungry, house the homeless?" I asked, waving a hand at the Riverwoods symbol hanging behind him.

"Jacob," he said, his jaw muscles tense and jumping beneath his skin. "Now is not the time to—"

"You can still stop this. You can talk to the city council, and keep them from taking—"

"You're always in your own little world," he said, shaking his head. "Nothing matters to Jace except Jace."

That stung. I swallowed hard. "Maybe that was true once, but I don't want to be—"

"You keep trying to bend everyone to your demands

instead of the other way around, and it's going to—"

I laughed, I couldn't help it. "Are you serious? When was the last time anyone ever bent for *me*?"

"When you called your brother in the middle of the night and made him pick you up!" he thundered.

The air vanished from my lungs, and I couldn't breathe for a second. He was right.

He swallowed audibly. "I'm sorry, Jacob. I didn't mean that. I know it was an accident, and I would never—"

"Eli," I said dully. "I know you wish he was the one who lived, and if I could do that for you—"

"No!" He sounded horrified. He paced a few steps and then knelt down at the edge of the stage. "Of course not. That's not it at all."

I didn't believe him. How could I? I would have traded everything to have Eli back. Why would my dad be any different?

I should have known better than to come and try to talk him into helping. My dad wouldn't listen to me. I was the fuck-up, the bad one, and I always would be.

I turned slowly, painfully, feeling every ache and break in my body, and started to walk away.

"I noticed the tires on the Jeep were looking worn," he called after me.

I stopped.

"Earlier that week. But I was running, trying to get to

a meeting on time. Everything was so crazy, and I thought it would slow down as soon as the expansion details were settled."

I turned to face him.

His shoulders slumped forward, and he looked defeated and weary. "I meant to mention it to you both when I got home, but I was busy and I . . . forgot." He scrubbed his hands over his face. "*I* got my son killed because I forgot." His mouth trembled with emotion, and then tears overflowed.

I rushed back to the stage, my eyes burning.

He reached down and pulled me close, his arms so tight around me that it almost hurt. "I'm so sorry, Jacob. If I'd warned you, told you and Eli to take the Jeep in and get the tires changed, none of this would have happened. You both would have probably been fine. I have to live with that. Not just Eli's death but the loss in your life, in Sarah's and your mother's. . . ." His voice broke. "That can't all be for nothing."

That's when I understood, finally. The expansion plans were his version of a memorial for Eli. "You're pushing for this because you want it to mean something for Eli? Dad, he wouldn't want that."

He released me to sit on the edge of the stage. "This was going to be his future," my dad said, holding a hand out in a gesture that incorporated the auditorium and the as-yet-unbuilt coffeehouse, community center, and whatever else they had in mind. "He should be remembered."

"Dad, he was going to try to stop the city," I said.

My dad stared at me, as if I were speaking gibberish.

"He wasn't trying to hurt anyone. He found out about what was happening and what Mr. Hauer was trying to do." I hesitated. "It bothered him. He thought it was wrong."

My father pushed himself up to his feet, wiping at his face. "I'm sure that's what that girl would like you to think, but it's not true. He would have talked to me about it."

I exhaled loudly in frustration. "That last night, when we were arguing about who got to take the car, you know what Eli said to me? 'Not everything is about you.'"

My dad sighed. "Jacob, I'm sure he didn't mean—"

"He didn't. He wasn't talking about me, not like that. I just didn't realize it then. He was scared and angry at himself for not living up to expectations. If it was hard for me always being the screwup, he had it even worse, always trying to be the good one."

"You're not a screwup," my dad began. "But you need to—"

"Just . . . Here, read this." I pulled Eli's notes from my back pocket.

After a moment of hesitation, my dad took the paper with the tips of his fingers, as if it might explode if handled too roughly.

"You read it and you tell me you think that all of this is okay. That it's worth it to 'bend the rules.'" I backed away from the stage.

"Jacob."

"Read it," I said, turning and heading up the aisle. "And tell me you still feel the same way. If you do, that's fine. Thera's family is going to get a copy too."

Maybe doing the right thing would win out, or maybe my dad's need to save face would force him to take action. Either way, I wasn't giving up without a fight. Not anymore.

THE GRASS ON ELI'S grave, barely poking through the dark mound of soil, was that pale, early spring green.

I stood well back from the fragile growth with Thera, on the existing lawn of the cemetery.

The late April afternoon sun was bright. It made the lilies that someone, probably Leah, had left glow a brilliant white, and it glinted off the shiny flecks in the granite of Eli's grave marker.

ELIJAH DAVID PALMER

SON, BROTHER, FRIEND

"Thanks for coming with me," I said to Thera. "I know you've got a lot going on with moving." A Riverwoods member, after hearing her story, had offered his rental property to Thera and her mom.

Thera threaded her fingers through mine. "It'll wait," she said. She gave my hand an encouraging squeeze and then let go.

I took a deep breath, then stepped forward to the edge of the new grass.

"So, um, hey, Eli." I stuffed my hands deeper into my pockets, feeling both foolish and the absurd need to get the words right. "I'm sorry it took me so long to come here. I wasn't ready."

Before, I'd needed to avoid any sign of Eli's death to keep from drowning in the questions, fears, and loss. I still had those things, but now I understood better that everyone else did too. And Eli's grave was a marker of someone who'd gone, but it was not all that was left of him.

"Dad isn't mad at you, if you're wondering. He was surprised, but I think he understood. And when he saw what Mr. Hauer had said to you . . ." My voice took on a sharpened edge. "Mr. Hauer isn't on the church council anymore. He resigned. I don't know if that was his idea or Dad's. But I'm glad. And Dad got the church council to give Thera and her mom a better offer."

I studied the line of dirt dividing Eli's plot from the ground where I was standing, like that doorway in the dream I'd had about him. "I wish you'd told me. I wish you could have talked to me about it. I wish I'd been the type of brother you could have come to with that kind of stuff." I swallowed hard over the lump in my throat, blinking back tears. "I know it's too late now, but I'm trying."

Thera moved to stand beside me and took my hand again.

I swiped at my eyes with the back of my free hand. "I gave Leah your Bible and the pictures I found in your room. She's still having a hard time, I think."

She'd burst into tears when I gave her the Bible and pictures, and then she'd hugged me.

"Leah helped us, Thera and me, with your yearbook page. She had lots of pictures I'd never seen. You wearing her Easter hat was my personal favorite." I shook my head with a laugh. "E, what were you thinking?"

I shifted my weight from foot to foot. The cast was finally off, but my leg ached when I stood for too long.

"The quotes were Thera's idea," I said, pulling her closer to me and wrapping my arm around her waist. She'd suggested that we get people to submit stories or facts about Eli—funny, sad, or touching. So his page was a half dozen carefully selected photos and then lots of quotes.

He liked the toothpaste cap on. (I helped Sarah with that one.)

Eli made sure I had enough to eat on our debate team trip.

He was a ruthless Scrabble player.

Eli cared when no one else did.

He hated it when you messed with his organizational system. I once flipped all the folders in his locker the wrong way to see how long it would take him to notice. The answer is: milliseconds.

Eli was the other half of me, in more ways than I realized. And I miss him.

Everyone loved the page. My mom had a copy made and framed. And pulling all of it together for a tribute sort of helped me, too, made me feel like I was *doing* something to honor Eli instead of just missing him.

As I stood there, I tried to think about anything and everything I would want Eli to know—how much better Sarah was doing with therapy, how my parents were talking about going too, how it looked like my former teammates might be headed to state without me and I didn't really mind because that felt like a lifetime ago—but it was all too much and not enough at the same time.

"Are we still going to meet up with Zach this afternoon?" Thera asked eventually, after I'd been quiet for a while.

"Yeah." I knew what she was trying gently to say: we would be late if we didn't leave soon. I was trying to find common ground with Zach and a couple of my other team friends, now that we no longer had baseball in common. Part of that was getting them to accept that Thera and I were together for real. It was a work in progress, but Thera was willing to try and the guys were slowly coming around to it.

Tonight, we were meeting Zach and Audrey and Derek and Lacey for pizza.

"It's hard to say good-bye," I said to Thera, dashing a hand under my eyes. "You know?"

"It's not good-bye. It's never really good-bye." She squeezed my hand tightly.

I stood there for a long moment in silence, feeling there was something else to say. Or maybe there was too much, and that was the problem.

"We're doing okay. We'd be better with you here, but I know that's not . . ." My voice broke, and I looked up at the sky, a perfect cloudless blue, until I get could my emotions in check to finish saying what I needed to say.

"I miss you," I said finally to Eli. "Every day for the rest of my life, however long that is. And I'm looking forward to seeing you again." I still didn't know what I believed for sure, but the words were both a closing and an expression of my deepest hope.

And that seemed exactly right.

ACKNOWLEDGMENTS

I grew up in a house where Sunday school lessons and *Star Trek* episodes were equally common discussion points. I owe an enormous debt to my dad, Pastor Stephen Barnes, for patiently listening to all my questions about churches, theology, and faith, both then and now. Thank you for always encouraging us to think as well as believe. (Also, I took lots of liberties with this story, as one does with fiction, so any blame belongs with me.)

Becky Douthitt, one of my college BFFs and a fellow PK, held my hand through this process all but literally. She read multiple ugly drafts, spent hours on the phone with me, and listened while I bounced (sometimes crazy) ideas off of her. To be a PK is to be a member of a unique club—whether we're angels or hell spawn—and I wanted to make sure I was doing it justice. Beck, thank you for your support on this and everything since we were eighteen. Love you!

ACKNOWLEDGMENTS

Linnea Sinclair is the very best critique partner who has EVER existed. She read every one of these chapters multiple times and sometimes on ridiculous timelines while I frantically revised and rewrote. She also came to visit when I was beyond stressed about how to fix this book. She and her husband took me to the beach and bought me French pastries. See? BEST EVER.

Christian Trimmer, my brilliant and very patient editor. We've worked together for years(!) on multiple books about ghosts and aliens. I never dreamed that writing about something I'd *actually experienced* (growing up in the church) would be so much harder. Thank you for giving me the chance to tell this story and for guiding me through the forest I couldn't see because of all the trees.

Suzie Townsend, my tireless and wise agent, thank you. Words cannot express how much I appreciate your calm confidence and expertise. I'm so incredibly grateful to have you as my advocate.

Amy Bland and Kimberly Damitz read early drafts, gave me feedback, and—this was huge—kept my spirits up during revisions. Thank you! I treasure our dinners together.

It takes a whole host of people to keep an author balanced and (mostly) sane. These are the people who feed me, remind me to laugh, make me leave the house occasionally, and still deem me a friend (or a family member in good standing) even after I've vanished down the rabbit hole for months: my patient husband, Greg Klemstein; my sister, Susan Barnes; my mom, Judy Barnes; Age, Dana, and Quinn Tabion; Ed, Deb, Lauren, and Eric Brown; and Michael, Jess, Grace, and Josh Barnes. My knitting club, particularly our fearless leader, Teagan A. My Starbucks community, especially Connie and Bud, and the baristas, Kiley, Sean, Jake, Caroline, Sharon, and both Sarahs. Thank you so much. I'm so grateful.